INSIDE *the* BEAUTIFUL INSIDE

Emily Bullock was born on the Isle of Wight where she spent most of her childhood. She worked in feature film production before taking an MA in creative writing at the University of East Anglia. She won the Bristol Short Story Prize and her stories have been included in many collections and broadcast on BBC Radio 4. Her debut novel, *The Longest Fight* was shortlisted for the Cross Sports Book Awards, and listed in *The Independent's* Paperbacks of the Year. She has a PhD from the Open University where she teaches creative writing. Emily lives in London but still dreams of the sea.

Emily Bullock

INSIDE the BEAUTIFUL INSIDE

Published in the UK by Everything with Words Limited
3rd Floor, Descartes House, 8 Gate Street,
London WC2A 3HP

www.everythingwithwords.com

Text copyright © Emily Bullock 2020

Emily Bullock has asserted hier right under the Copyright, Design and Patents Act 1988 to be identified as the author of this work.

This books is sold subject to the condition that it shall not, by way of trade or otherwise, be lent, resold, hired out, or otherwise circulated without the publisher's prior consent in any form of binding or cover other than that in which it is published and without a similar condition, including this condition, being imposed on the subsequent purchaser.

Printed and bound in Great Britain by
CPI Group (UK) Ltd, Croydon CRO 4YY

A CIP catalogue record for this book is available from the British Library.

ISBN 978–1–911427–19–3

For Carole and Del

PEARSE STREET BRANCH
BRAINSE SRÁID PIARSACH
TEL: 6744888

Atlantic Ocean, 1782

'You saved me.'

'We'll save each other yet, Fletcher.'

'Something glinted in the water...'

'Hard fall from the rigging.'

'You caught me, James.'

'What any would do.'

'Tell me again.'

'Of the warm sea – feels like summer beer? Breadfruit low hanging, plump – women – oh, beautiful enough – make a man's balls shrink.'

'Paradise.'

'Plenty for all. You'll find a love – will bathe with you – eat with you – live side by side – in battle she'll fight with you.'

'Should like that...'

'Fletcher – stay awake – have hold of me.'

'Will they find us?'

'Cambridge – not the fastest ship – good for us –'

'Don't let go.'

'– rope will hold – listen for the bell.'

'Paradise – in this life, James?'

'Promise it – won't let go.'

I

MAN OVERBOARD

1

Deptford, 1800

Is it day yet? Hard to tell in this curtained berth at the mission. I lie on my back. Darkness lies back on me, thick as tar. Stuck to the bed.

I pinch the skin on my knuckles. Awake, not dead then. Either way they'll find me with boots on, coat on. The buttons dig into my chin. I'd like to see the man could take my uniform from me. If ever I do, he'll likely be from a place such as this.

The Seaman's Mission is the black depths. The Seaman's Mission is my sanctuary.

I don't know how I came to be here.

I do know but I don't want to remember. Not that swirling hell. Not that stink of death. Onwards, to blue water for me. I've a sea monster to slay – that thinks itself a man, struts as a man, shouts as a man. It lives my life! I punch the straw bedding. I must return to ship, the land is no good for me, the city is eating me – that can't be true, it's the bad beef pie, it's the booze, only the pie was all swede and gravy and the rum was watered down.

I sit up. Head knocking the bunk above.

I'm really feeling much better.

I lie down.

Death is waiting for me on the other side of the curtain.

Or is this the dream?

No sooner am I down the Mission stairs than my new mess mates are there to fetch me. Usually I like to choose my own mates when I meet a fresh crew but they seem a jolly pair, and I've just come from a hot smothered dream, and feel in no mood to set them right. I had a mess mate once... felt sorry for the pup, even saved him from the sea. Well, didn't he grow into a sly dog.

I've no use for mates now, let this lot have me. Rather a hammock and crow's foot biscuits than the dead air of the Mission. I set a brisk pace, swing my arms, happy that I'm off to sea again.

A carriage, horses, plump fellows bouncing beside me.

Almost a ship. Back and forth we go. Up and down.

Street and dust.

Can't see what's out there. Nothing is still. Nothing's been still for many a month.

Close my eyes.

Use my hands as anchor, clutched fists in my pockets.

The journey passes as journeys do.

The carriage stops. They make a show of holding open the door, taking my arm, helping me to the ship. Which isn't needed but strikes me as a friendly gesture.

So, I'm onboard. Only yesterday I thought I'd never put out of harbour again, and now my new mates are leading me through the ship. Let the wind blow, let the currents run, I'll find what I'm hunting far out across the waves.

Of course, I'm grateful to be here, but it's a strange place, dark and sodden. A seventy-four gun ship of the third rate, going by the size of these decks. I can usually tell from her shadow but I don't recall catching sight of her before stepping below.

The sailors about this place have shaved heads. Must have been lice. Some ships get like that after many months at sea. It would never happen on Captain Bligh's watch; too fond of the vinegar.

I thought the Mission meant to keep me from a commission. I misjudged them.

Thank God no one there got the thought to lock me up in a madhouse. I've seen them do that to troublesome old salts. I'm not old yet but I've been feeling rougher than the last sea-biscuit in the barrel.

This is just what I need, time at sea. Though how we got from Deptford to Portsmouth so quick I don't recall. A fast carriage, fresh horses can do it in less time than you'd think these days.

It's the fever stealing hours from me.

Losing time used to be fatal at sea; a sailor could get too far off course to navigate his way home. They have clocks now that keep ship's time. I've seen them for myself. I don't suppose this old girl has one. She's broken down like privateers have sucked the marrow from her bones. There's some about this place, lying on the deck, look all skin and bone. Flog the cook. Him there has a bleeding sore on his scalp. Damn the surgeon.

My skin itches.

Dirty lice.

Getting a bad feeling.

Guts are churning.

They march me on. The deck runs and runs.

Something's sour – stinks like a plague of rats died in the ballast. Men lie about like there's no work to be done. Where's the watch? How deep down in the hold are we? Can't hear the sea's heartbeat. That lamp, shining too white, burns me. That crow at the window stares into me. Hands dig into my arms.

I'm a marine not a prisoner.

Left standing with your cock in your hand, that's you, James Norris.

I'll not answer, not now I'm on my way again.

The crow pecks at the glass. Only the Captain's rooms have windows; why are we going there?

Sign me up, what else do I have? But don't take me to the Captain. I'm not fit to be seen. What's left of me? I've got no sides to hold anything in. Look how my arms and legs shimmer. If my new mess mates step away, I'll splash to the floor.

I'm a drowning man. I'm drowning, man! Nothing but spit comes out.

Those doors up there, what's behind them?

Am I watched?

The boards beneath my feet are rotten; they'll not survive the pitch and roll of a storm.

Down to the lower deck. Least those doors can't spy me here. No hammocks up yet, always hard to tell night from day down below.

There's another door.

I'm not liking the look of this.

I've signed up with a bad fucking lot. Not a decent red uniform between them. I'm the only man with his boots and buttons ready for inspection. But she's a big ship. Can't even reach the planks above. A grand old lady.

They drag me on.

'Do you think I'm green?' I say, trying to pull away. They've got quite the pinch on me.

That door, all carved wood, big locks, is getting closer. Two sailors stand side by side in front of it, looking like some double headed dog monster.

'Listen, you bastards.' I try to prise their fingers off my arms. 'Don't I know my way round a ship?'

They laugh at that, but they're not so jolly as I first thought. Four of them now, and me – not best odds. But all about this place looks like misery kicked them in the arse. The cracked wood, the rat shit, and straw – no sailor lets straw lie on the floor. They must have had a bad bad voyage of it. This is my last chance, too late once they have me through that door... anything could be on the other side.

One of the sailors in the doorway beckons. 'Don't fight it,' he says.

Why would he say that? My father used to say that. I turn my head, twist my neck but there's no clock to set on this ship. Time is slipping again. If we sail soon perhaps I'll be saved. I have to leave behind that darkness, those dreams... the face that waits for me there.

'Seaward, boys,' I call.

It's not professional to be escorted like this, even if it is in jest. And it isn't like me to allow it. But I'm sweating, my legs shake a little, fever burns under my nails. I've not slept enough. My body's thick with waking. My new mess mates pull away, leave me standing there like I'm pissing into the wind. Slow, if only everything would slow. But I don't like to be late. Captain Bligh never tolerated lateness. Everything had to be in the correct place at the correct time. These sailors are expecting me. They take hold of my arms. Maybe they've served with Bligh.

'My old captain...' They love sentimental tales do sailors. Only it's a tale I'll not tell to anyone. Bligh and me. Suppose I don't look too well in it.

They're taking me through that door. I don't want to enter. What's waiting on the other side? Tell me that.

Tell me something.

The fever scorches me, hot as a fired cannon. They'll have to let go soon or I'll melt their flesh. They shove me. Caught by the two sailors now, fixed tight. Dragged inside the door.

Black as a bilge hole.

Black enough to make a man forget who he is. But I'll never forget what I'm after.

I brace my arms against the frame. One grabs my neck, forces it forward. The other kicks at my legs. They'll not get me in there.

For a moment, in that darkness, I think I see my father standing up ahead. I remember how it was back then. Only seventeen, thinking I was a man. A young buck hobbled by having an old goat so close. He's the reason I became a marine. All the way to the docks, signing up with a fishing boat, sailing off the Boston coast, further into the Atlantic, praying to any god who'd listen to let the English find me, let the navy have me. Through seasickness, through storms, I asked myself the same questions: What are you James Norris? Your father's shadow, less of a man than a lesser man? Or are you a fighter? Don't you want to be something?

The English boarded us on the second month at sea. They called out for any not free born. I was English made if not born – it was a small lie, only what they wanted to hear.

I became a marine that day, answered their cry, Come boys, who's for blue water?

I shake my head. That's all done with, I made my choices. A man can't win a fight against the past as it is what it is, no changing it. But the past has a way of lashing out, slicing you open – it wants you to bloody brawl.

I feel the same now as I did when a boy, on board a strange ship. Sweat sticks the shirt to my back. Someone take me to sea. And all I have to do is follow them, walk through this darkness. How can I do anything else?

I shout out, 'Come boys, who's for blue water?'

2

They say I'm mad.
I say they're mad.
I lost the flip.
That's me locked up in Bethlem Hospital.
'Come boys, who's for Bedlam?'

3

It was many days earlier that I first arrived in this place, although I didn't know where I was then. Now, a marine should always have his bearings but I'll be forgiven if a chill had left me low, and no man gets good kip at the Seaman's Mission. All that aside I was too long on land, that's what was wrong with me.

Time to fix my compass points.

There are many rooms in Bethlem Hospital, although I've only been in two.

There are six windows in this room, which is as long as a gallery. I'm standing in the middle of it. Four bars at each window, thirty-six bars in all, forty if you count the grill on the door. One hundred and forty-six flagstones (forty-eight counting those that are missing); I've stepped on each one. The mice come and go, but I've my particular favourites, the one with the bent tail and the other with a squeak sounds like a lady's sneeze. I crouch down, watch little Bent Tail darting between the straw beds. He's quick but comes every day so it seems he's not found a way out yet.

There's laughter, a whistle, out in the passageway. I shoo Bent Tail out of sight. The wild dogs tearing up the place out there, that's the keepers. Two of them, far as I can tell: Fleet and Rodley.

I've yet to look them in the eye. But Fleet has the cleanest boots, hardly a patch or a nail in them, so really we have one boss and one keeper.

And the men, the crew as I call them, well I mustn't forget them even though some seem to have forgotten themselves. Seventy-two... Ha, if that isn't two men to every bar. Don't suppose they'll divide us up like a gun crew. Really there are seventy-three men if you count that one in the darkest corner. He's small, pale-faced but dark hair pokes out from his chest, arms and legs. He laughs and giggles as he holds his hands to the grey light from the window. The black fur and dark lines on his face make him look like a long lost castaway but he's much younger than that. I take a man as I find him, and this one's only a boy. That takes it back to seventy-two.

Bent Tail scampers back and forth over my boots as I cross the room. He's trying to tie a bowline knot out of me, trying to capsize me, and what with the uneven flagstones, he nearly does. I place my feet carefully.

From a distance these men could be anyone. I try not to mark all their faces or names. I call them crew but I know they're not – we're landlocked.

Only when I've set my compass will I know my course. No sailing into the wind this time – from storm to hurricane – mission to madhouse. I must plot carefully if I'm to get what I want.

Footsteps echo in the passage.

Some of the crew begin to slide back against the bricks, or burrow into the straw. They make animals of themselves: mewing like a birthing cat, barking, smacking monkey lips. Well, I'm no beast and here I'll stand. Let them come to me.

Fleet leads the way in his shiny boots, Rodley files in behind him. Fleet is shorter than Rodley but his arms and neck are knotted with muscles. He could crack heads easy as eggshells. And he must have had some fights. His nose is broken, flattened at the end like an oar.

Fleet beats a ladle against the bars. 'Stand back, lunatics. Today is meat day.'

He couldn't have said anything more likely to make us all push and shove. Him and Rodley stand with a bucket between them. Steam rises, the smell of flesh and blood drifts through the room.

The crew clump together, more arms and legs than an octopus. Like me they taste the fog of meat, some with tongues hanging out. Rodley ladles up, and it's been so many days since there was broth that it takes me a while to dig in the straw and find my cup.

There's only me and Parrot Boy left. Rodley scrapes all through the kettle, comes up with half a ladleful. He drips it into my cup.

'Would you know it, we're all out.' He drops the empty bucket on Parrot Boy's head.

The boy's sharp elbows jut out like plucked wings. 'All out. All out.' He backs away, knocks against the door, turns about, flops down on the straw.

Rodley takes a loaf of bread out from his shirt, bites off a chunk. He's tighter than any purser I've ever sailed with, eating rations meant for us. Chews it around, wipes his lips, takes another bite.

I stand by the door, hands about the cup. Steaming hot, meat too. I breathe it in.

Rodley spits a bit of grit at me, offers Fleet the bread.

Fleet pushes it away. 'Don't know how you eat that filth, lad.'

'Don't cost nothing.'

'Always got your nose up the apothecary's crack. Few pennies must have dropped out of there by now.'

Rodley takes another bite. 'I ain't going to be stuck a keeper all my life.'

'You spend too much time dreaming. Get a wife, that'll keep you busy.'

Rodley grins. 'I don't pay for that in here neither.'

'You'll pay for that bloody bucket if we don't get it back to the kitchen.' Fleet lifts it off Parrot Boy's head.

Parrot Boy gulps, his head bobs. Fleet and Rodley step over him, laughing.

The boy must only be about twelve. I raise the cup to my face; there's some beef in there all right. Twelve: that's old enough to set to sea. But he's a thin, sickly-looking sort, just like my brother William – though William could eat as much as me. I dip my finger in the broth, a good salty tang to it. William's a half-brother, his mother was never my mother; I used to tell him that when he snivelled or whined – only what any older brother would do.

William was a dreamy one. Once he turned the barn into a new land, rivers, forests, castles. Must have taken him all day. No one noticed – it wasn't that sort of world – but when William took me by the hand, led me through, I saw it too.

Parrot Boy blinks. Those eyes are watery and dark. His hair is lank, patches of scalp showing on his head: a half-drowned, scrap of a thing. I push my cup into Parrot Boy's hands. He stares, steam collecting on his beak of a nose.

'Don't let it go cold, you runt.'

I stride over straw, push back the crew in my way. My gut is tight as a mainsail. I lick my lips, steady myself, hand on the wall. Anyway, the keepers probably pissed in the soup bucket, or worse.

4

Is that spring I taste? I lean an elbow on the high ledge of the middle window where the angled walls allow a narrow view of the yard. A popular porthole. The stone is worn yellow, moulded like butter with the handprints of a thousand men or more.

They bring more men every week, but no one has been taken out. Eighty-one.

Not much to do once I've counted the flagstones, bars, windows, and crew. Every day drags its tail into one long dog watch afternoon.

My head sinks into the crook of my arm. The chill air from the yard scratches my neck.

I shouldn't be here.

Something knocks against my ankle. An old man lies on the floor, straw and dirt stick to his cheeks and hair. He gives a merry wink, seems not to care he's so low down in the filth. So, why should I?

'Morning,' I say.

'Name's Hooke. Call me Old Man Hooke, most do.'

I shrug.

'You don't seem the sort not to call a body something, nor not to be called something in return.'

Old Man Hooke might have lost use of his legs but he hasn't lost any words.

'I'm James Norris.'

'They fetched me here a few days past,' he says. 'How long for you?'

'Place it at two months.' I stretch my neck, can't see far. 'If I could see the sun and stars I'd be able to give you a better reckoning of it.'

'A marine, that's you.'

I tip my head back against the wall to get a better look at him. He's still smiling, wrinkles about his eyes, only one in this place to hold a smile.

'How do you know what I am?'

'Wide stance.' Old Man Hooke pats my boot. 'Only man in here who walks straight on this slopping floor. A soldier of the sea.'

I laugh (first time I've heard that in here). There's no echo in this brick and stone hole; it fades to nothing. 'A fever sent me here, that's all. Tropics gets into the blood. Scorches you to the soul.'

'All that's behind you. It is the waiting gets to most in here, but we all must wait.' He lifts his chin from the floor, points at the window. 'Have you been to the yard yet?'

'No.'

He blows away a spider that scuttles too close. 'Keepers must be waiting for fair weather, they take us sometimes... if we're good. You'll get some air out there.'

'Maybe.' I wish he wouldn't lie so close; looking down on him seems to shrink the cell, making me a trapped giant.

Won't let myself think about the crumbling deckhead crushing down on me, the walls squeezing about my neck. I rub my nose, open my nostrils to suck in more air. The sharp burn of piss nearly drops me to my knees.

'You'll get used to it but don't get too used to it.' He gives another wink. 'I'm a fool but an old one, so I've learned a thing or two.'

I crouch down below the window, shoo Bent Tail away from Old Man Hooke's chin. 'I need to learn all about this place; are you that man?'

Old Man Hooke wobbles a loose tooth with his tongue. His eyes roll back like he's trying to see behind his head towards the door. 'Keep all that you've got about you. Keep clean. Keep quiet.'

I've listened to worse advice. He beckons me closer. I hold my knees, lean in.

He whispers, 'They taken anything from you yet?'

'Time.'

He nods. 'Today my legs, another my hands.'

But he's not your usual lank-sleeve, or one-legged sailor sort. I see his hands, I see his legs. 'Seems careless to be losing so many bits of yourself.'

'They can work away at me all they like. A year is all I must do, I know this.'

'Tell me more.'

'You seem a sensible sort, James Norris, so I don't mind telling you all I've learned of Bethlem.' He pulls at his ear. I kneel down beside him to better catch his words. 'They have a year to keep us then they must let us go. But only if you stay in your senses. Anger the keepers, lark about, laugh at the surgeon, spit at the apothecary, and they'll sign you over to incurables.' He checks over his shoulder. 'My wife always comes banging on the gates for me when my year is done.'

He smoothes himself down, looks back to me. 'They'll test you, James Norris. It will not be fair sailing.'

He rolls away.

A year.

A year is all I must do.

An out-pension might be waiting. I'll be back in the marines soon. There's one out there, I hope he's waiting too, hope he sweats through each night knowing I'm coming for him but not knowing when. I know when.

Ten months to go.

Even if they take keep for this place it can't be much. I've pissed away more on a week's shore leave: a drink for the house, a song from the lasses, a bone for the dog, a ride up and down the cobbles in a fine hire carriage, new ribbons for some pretty bit. When I get out I'll buy silver buckles for me and my mess mates. Golden ribbons – that's what I bought for Ruth. I usually bought red, no mistaking what sort they are when they accept such a gift. But Ruth had this brown hair, thick as rope, with golden threads like she'd been licked by the sun. Gold, that was the colour for Ruth.

Oh Ruth, I still itch for you, you pretty, green-eyed, small-boned as a blackbird, treacherous bitch...

There are no trials I can go through in here could be worse than where I've already been.

5

Today Old Man Hooke has no arms. I watched him chase a cup around the floor with his chin but there wasn't much sport in it.

I hold the chipped pottery to his mouth. He sips, gives me a wink. 'Just the thing.' He smacks his lips together.

I hear shouting from the passage. We've already had our rations. 'Is it yard day?'

Old Man Hooke coughs a little, licks a dribble from his chin. 'First comes the washing then the airing.'

He thinks himself an old shirt or pair of breeches, soft-boiled egg that he is. I watch the door. He takes another sip, head bobbing.

I put down the cup. 'I'll ask the keepers when we can go to the yard.'

He lowers his head, gently nudges the cup away. 'You've no business with any in here but Haslam.'

'Why's that?'

'Haslam's the one signed you in,' he says. 'You'd do well to pay him attention. He's the one gets to sign you out.'

Old Man Hooke coughs, and I push the cup to him. He takes a sip. 'Thank you,' he says.

'I know what it is to thirst.'

He nods, arms so still it's easy to think they really are gone, hands disappeared inside long sleeves. He settles himself against the wall. I sit beside him.

He prods my boot with his foot. 'Think only on what waits for you outside these walls.'

'I do... There's a man out there owes me. I mean to collect.'

'He has your money?'

'I've nothing to my name.'

'He has your wife?'

'Not married.'

'Your child?'

'No child.'

'Then he owes you nothing.'

I shake my head. 'You have it all wrong, Old Man Hooke.'

'I've only what you say.'

I throw the cup to the floor, take Old Man Hooke by the shoulders, lean in close. 'My word... I've still got that. *He* owes me everything and that's what I mean to collect.'

Old Man Hooke gives me a wink. 'Good, remember how you long to be away. Remember what I say. Anger the keepers, lark about, laugh at the surgeon, spit at the apothecary, and they'll sign you over to incurables. Do your best to disappear for the time they have you.'

He shuffles up with his back against the wall, scuttles over to a corner of the room furthest from the door. The sodden April light makes a shadow of him.

The keepers are getting closer. I stand up. They laugh, heckle each other, voices thick and muffled as if we're trapped underwater in here. Maybe they are only passing, off to sink their tot of beer and rum. The key clatters in the lock, the door opens.

A fat man dressed in black stands beside Fleet and Rodley. He points to something in the room. He paces, riding boots clopping on the boards. A third chin threatens to blossom over his white neckerchief. Clergy maybe. God's messenger to the mad. That's all this crew needs.

See how the men wash back against the walls and each other like rats clambering to be away. Not that it bothers me to notice this. Not at all. I'm a marine. *Per mare per terram* – it doesn't say nothing about *per* Bethlem Hospital for the mad. Here we're all better off not being seen. Even a fool can speak the truth, and I plan to pay heed to Old Man Hooke's ramblings.

The fat man flaps his black coat, stamps his foot. 'Clean from the dirty. Violent from the harmless.'

Rodley is close at his side. 'Yes, Surgeon Crowther.'

Fleet thumbs Rodley.

The surgeon waits outside the door. The keepers enter, Fleet and Rodley. They've not had a drop of booze, they are white-lipped and black-eyed with sobriety. They lock the door, forming a battle line. Fleet's face shines as much as his new boots, slick with sweat, sickly white as land lovers are. He wears a collarless shirt, jacket blackened up with soot, and a yellow neckcloth. There's no uniform but Rodley dresses as he does.

Fleet yells, 'Wash time, you filthy bastards.'

Parrot Boy echoes the call, 'Wash time. Wash time.'

Now this is new. What I wouldn't give for a splash of water, a wash and mend day just like onboard. But Old Man Hooke's words are fresh in my head. *Anger the keepers, lark about, laugh at the surgeon, spit at the apothecary, and they'll sign you over to incurables*. I'm not sure what the incurables is but don't suppose it's good.

I keep to the wall. Over the slope of the window, the women take a turn in the yard. And I watch them because I'm a man not a lunatic. The swish of their brown skirts on the cobbles, the flap of loose hair, reminds me for a moment of being up on deck, the mainsail rustling with a harbour breeze, the line to land fastening us like an outstretched hand, and the dock women have brought with them the earthy taste of their mouths and the salty slickness between their legs.

Each in turn as she passes in the yard lifts her face and each has the same small nose, the same wide eyes, the same heart-shaped chin as Ruth. All those Ruths staring up at me.

But the keepers are in the middle of the room now, there's no bucket, no water. The crew scatter to the corners. I take my hands out from under my arms. A marine must always be ready for battle, though they'll get no rise from me.

What do I care that the keepers have grabbed Parrot Boy? He turns his head, hoping they meant to take someone else instead. I saw a lorikeet in Tahiti once taken that way by dogs, and I still don't know why it didn't try to fly, why it sat and waited until the teeth tore into it before fluttering its wings. What do I care that Parrot Boy is screaming because they've ripped him from his nest against the wall? Sweet Jesus, can he scream. Parrot Boy thrusts out his palms as if they are bayonets, but it doesn't stop the keepers from surrounding him.

'Time to wash you clean,' Fleet says.

'Wash you clean. Wash you clean,' Parrot Boy chirrups.

Fleet puts an arm about his chest, pins Parrot Boy's wings. He whimpers, tries to flap. Fleet tightens his grip, lifts the boy off the floor. Rodley laughs, not because he hates the boy but because he hates himself – now that's a snake with a most poisonous bite. Fleet carries Parrot Boy squawking and wriggling to the door.

Rodley calls over his shoulder, 'This is the Palace Beautiful, and we have a duty to keep it so.'

'Well said, man.' The surgeon nods. 'Shaving and bleeding – cleans them inside and out.'

The palace beautiful; outside it might have been deserving of that name, once. All of London must have seen its stone pineapples, its unicorn on the low pier gates, its grand coat of arms. But smell it. Touch it. It rots.

Rodley locks the door behind them.

Parrot Boy must learn, comes a time in every boy's life when he sees the world outside of himself, let's go of hopes of kingdoms and soldiers, sees his treasures as the sticks and pebbles and feathers that they are, and hates himself for the fool he was only moments before who knew no better. Maybe some washing will make a man of him.

I turn to the window.

Never one to help a fellow out, were you, James Norris?

I rub a fist against my ear. This place is full of echoes.

Outside, the echo from the women's boots makes it sound like they are treading on glass. Their breath weaves lacework as they walk in circles about the square yard. Order and discipline, that's what every good ship needs. On punishment day, at six bells in the forenoon watch, the order is given, All hands to witness punishment. Justice is done for all to see – Parrot Boy must have done something to deserve such treatment.

A year (less three months served) is all I have to do.

I've been at sea for longer than that, no real hardship. I'll lean against this window; got a little thin without drill duty, musket cleaning, to keep me strong. I've still years left in me, signed on for a fifth-five. I'm not the sort to be pensioned off, open an inn or plough a field – not me.

A year (less three months served) is all I have to do. Let Parrot Boy's mother worry over him.

I lean against the wall, strain to peer up into the sky. There it is, just what I need to lift me, drawn out on the clouds – a body, the slope of hips, the rise of a belly – my Ruth, as she was back when we were each other's. Ruth, that morning in the small room above the inn at Portsmouth, was curled on her side, eyes open but not looking at anything. She knew I was watching. She grabbed my hand, drew me close against her. 'Let me tell you a secret, James – something I've never told – you want to know where I am. Inside. Don't look confused, James – in the inside of myself. It is beautiful in there.'

Ruth had smiled, not wanting any answer from me. I thought of my mother back then, and how I'd never known her, only those months she carried me inside her, but I knew her as a feeling of warmth inside myself like a southerly wind after days of stillness at sea. And so I believed Ruth when she told me this, although Ruth is a cock-sucking liar.

The women are led out of the yard. The emptiness of the cobbles hurts my eyes. Staring down into the mud, everything tips onto its side.

*

I am twelve years old. Lying flat on my front, up in the hayloft. Dust and husks skip in the air about me. I'm supposed to be turning the hay but I must have fallen asleep in the warm gloom.

Arrows of daylight cross the loft floor. I was dreaming of a battle, leading the cry out on a bright white horse, men cheering. Rub my eyes. There's a creaking noise behind me. I roll over. And she's there, in the far corner, under the eaves.

My mother sits in a rocking chair. I shuffle forwards. Her hair is the colour of hazelnuts, her face pink and faded like the little painting my father has. She rocks, wraps her hands over her middle. I bulge inside her, pressing to get out. I wouldn't be so fast if I knew how my birth would be her death. I stand behind her. She sings of many things: how they found her in the pond, how I kept her afloat until they could haul her out, how she fought long enough to push me free.

I can't hear her words, but I feel the rush of air from her lips; the tune dances on my skin. A wasp crawls over my fingers. Want to brush it away but can't move. The yellow and black hairs bristle.

As I stand behind her, I wonder if she remembers that day, her last, or if it is only a tale she sings. I hear a different story from the women in the cottages where we live. I'm a devil about these alleys and doorways. The milk's soured – was James Norris dipped his finger in it. The pig has eaten her litter – was James Norris lingered too long at the sty.

The wasp thrusts its sting into the thin skin on the back of my hand. I let it sting me again. Mustn't move.

My mother pets the me that's inside her. She doesn't know the boy behind her. Why won't she look at me? It's the baby that tells her she is dead and I am not. The baby that tells her I have to leave again. The baby that answers her goodbye, my mouth is too full of snot and tears to reply.

6

Nights here are the longest. They swallow me. In Bedlam all is darkness. Darkness sticks me to the straw. Darkness hides me from myself. Darkness so heavy, it's hard to breathe. So many things lurk in the depths. They swirl and glint like fish darting just below the surface.

The scratching in the walls, no worse than rats onboard. The squeak of sweaty skin – Parrot Boy lies a few bodies over; he likes to pull at his own feathers – it must itch now his hair grows back, though his voice is still missing. I miss a hammock, nothing better for comfort. But I've got myself a decent spot: away from the door, so I'll never be stumbled on unawares, away from the window, to keep the straw dry, up against the far wall so I've only crew starboard and stern.

Something scampers across my foot. I think it's some man come too close before I feel the brush of fur on my hand. Bent Tail squeaks, sits close to my face. He wants to know if I'm awake. I give a little nod. He darts to a hole in the wall, crooked tail snagging on the bricks as he scurries away.

'Come back soon,' I say.

'Hoy,' a voice whispers from the wall. 'Who's there?'

Could be a trick, the keepers or some other plotter. I crawl a little closer, lay my head beside the hole. 'Who wants to know?'

'Nobody.'

I'm not one for games, too many fools here who don't know any rules. I plump the straw beside me, get ready to roll back.

The whisper comes again, 'Nobody is what they call me.' A finger works its way through the gap between the bricks. 'You don't need to tell me your name.'

'True.'

The finger waves then slides back out of sight. A coughing disturbs the lime and mortar, and I think I'll get some peace again but the voice whispers, 'Hoy, who's there?'

'Shut up, will you.' I shake my head but I don't roll away.

'I was hoping someone else might hear me.'

I stretch out, put my hands behind my head. 'No one awake here but me.'

'It's taken months to scrape this opening. It was my first plan to get out, but the walls are too thick and I've nothing but a spoon.'

'You're out for trouble, are you?'

'Out for freedom, friend.'

'Friend – that's not a word to be free with.'

'I don't mean offence, but I'm in need of one.... This new plan of mine, it will take two.'

'Don't say more. I'm doing my time then I'm gone.'

'That's what Parrot Boy thought.'

'What do you know of him?'

'No one can put his squawk back.'

Listening to voices in walls; Old Man Hooke didn't need to warn me about that. 'Leave me to do my time in peace.'

'They won't let you. They... shh.'

All goes quiet. I press my hand to the wall; feels cold, wet. I shake my head. Lunatics each and everyone.

The voice is back, 'They're coming your way – haven't got long. You're wrong about getting out. They won't let it happen. Got to break out. That's the only way... They're coming.'

A streak of light shows port side. The door surfaces from the darkness. Someone sails in the passageway, hunting. Shadows fall through the bars, onto sleeping crew. Tonight they come for us ninety-three.

Click and turn of the key. A keeper opens the door, another man follows him – too thin to be the surgeon. A yellow sickness flows with them. The keeper holds a thick staff in his hand, beating it against his thigh – it's Rodley, the same outward jut of his chin. He's a man always straining to see what is next for him. The heavy stick must be in place of company.

They bring a false dawn with them. Crew turn, mutter, yawn and cough. A fart. Rodley pokes and prods with his stick. The other man is searching, bending low, the lamp swaying, dancing shapes around us: a couple of resurrection men mining for bodies. They'll not put a rope around my neck, yank me from my sleeping place. I always hoped to be buried at sea, no digging me up, cutting me up, they'd have to fight the fishes for me.

Rodley and the man sway in the light. After a moment I begin to think I'm swaddled in my hammock, swinging low in the fo'c'sle, and the lumps of strangers are really my mess mates, my regiment. And there would be some peace in letting my mind drift back to those old times, to stay there... Every man of the sea knows the dangers of drifting. But what if Hooke is wrong? And if there's no getting out – how will I take what's owed to me? What if they come for me like they came for Parrot Boy? I grow weaker each day, they might get the better of me – but not yet.

Every marine must come out fighting.

The light touches my feet. I see who stands with Rodley. The apothecary. Haslam, the man who signed me in. He slips between the beds of straw, cloak fluttering. He hasn't found what he's searching for. But he's about to find me. His face is a mask, on a mask, on a mask. Maybe deep enough down there's nothing but blackness, like staring into Bedlam itself. He must choose those masks each morning like selecting a coat from the rack.

I lie still until the lamp drops its light on my face. I grab Haslam's arm. Rodley doesn't see his man slip under.

I lift my face to Haslam. 'It's a mistake. I had a fever is all.'

He pulls against me. 'Now you're well?' The low light makes his eyes and mouth dark; he looks like a skull. 'Warm, fed, and ready to depart?'

Here's a man who longs to be more than he is, I say to myself. Didn't I know such a man always wished himself into the captain's hat? Look where getting too close to him got me!

'I'm a working man, never asked for charity.' He needs to know I'm used to better company than this. 'When I sailed with Bligh. Yes, Captain Bligh. He used to say to me...'

'A seafaring man.' Haslam rubs his bright white collar. He's thinking something over.

When I have him on the hook, then he'll believe me... might even bring forward my release.

Haslam tilts forward. 'Captain Bligh, you say?'

'Why yes,' I answer. 'Do you know him too?'

'Of him and his exploits. A hero for our times. Or was once.'

'That he is. He used to say to me –'

'Were you on the Bounty?' Like a young boy at his first lay, he comes too soon.

'Well –' If I lie he's sure to check; my record can be found. Then what might he do?

Haslam wants to hear about that and only that. 'Wouldn't it be a tale to tell at the club? The mutiny on the Bounty – how did it begin?'

I scratch my chin. 'A round-robin would be the traditional way –'

'You were on the Bounty?'

I need this man to believe I speak only the truth. 'HMS Cambridge is where I first sailed with Captain Bligh.'

Haslam stands up. 'Keeper.'

I've already vanished from his head. I'm afraid to hold up my hand and look right through myself.

Rodley hears him, places his boot on my gut. 'All well, Mr Haslam?'

Haslam unpeels my hand. 'All well, but not with this man.'

Rodley lifts his staff to strike. I seize it, haul him down. Let him see he's not got the better of me. Haslam's lamp swings back. I grunt, let go. Rodley steps away like he's landed a blow. He's got the sense not to try for a real hit. I only hope it's too dark for Rodley to pick me out for a set-to in daylight. I don't need to carry about the weight of his revenge on my shoulders. I've enough of my own load to carry.

'Open up, keeper,' Haslam calls out again.

Rodley kicks the water bucket out of his way, spilling half our ration, in his hurry to serve Haslam. I wonder if Haslam knows any of the keepers' names but sets himself apart by not using them, or if he's never known. Either way he's an ignorant bastard.

The bolt screeches, drops into place. Another night in here. But how long before they come for me?

What if Haslam is as blind as he seems?

And if Old Man Hooke is wrong about the year... Well, I need more than one shot in my musket. More than one out.

Won't be shipwrecked here.

I reach out, run my hand along the wall. 'Nobody.'

'Thank the Lord. I heard Haslam's voice – thought you were done for.'

'Tell me the plan.'

'Soon.'

'Now,' I say.

'You might go without me, then what would I do?'

'No need to whisper, speak like a man.'

'A chill's laid me low for weeks.'

'What if you get sicker without the chance of telling me?'

'You didn't seem so keen before. What do you want?'

'Out of here,' I say.

'But what is it you want?'

'To kill a man.'

'Who?'

'Fletcher Christian.'

'Who?'

I laugh. 'You must be the only man in England doesn't know *him*.'

'They call me Nobody – there are many things I no longer know.'

This seems like truth to me. I will listen to Old Man Hooke, abide by his warning... until I hear Nobody's plan – then I'll see which way the tide takes me.

I ask, 'If you won't tell me through the wall, how will you tell me?'

'Soon they will have to let us into the yard. I'll tell you all then.'

'How will I know you?'

'I'll have a blanket on my shoulders,' he whispers. 'I'll lift it over my head.'

'Keep well, Nobody. We have plans to make.'

I lie down on the straw, loosen my boots but leave them on (if the mice didn't take them someone else would). I haven't said that name, Fletcher Christian, since the last time I saw him – ten or more years past – little by little hatred has grown inside me as little by little my life got worse. I want all he owes me, but he can't give me that, can't give me Ruth, can't give me my youth, can't take away those memories of battle.

He who has no faults is not born.

I said it to Nobody, I'll say it again, 'I'll find Fletcher Christian and I'll kill him.'

And not with a bayonet or knife. I hold up my hands, a ghostly outline in the darkness. My hands is how I'll do it. I rest my palms on my face, feel the warmth of my breath. I want the heat of Fletcher Christian's blood to run cold against my skin.

7

I've left footprints on a glacier.

I've seen the sun burst out of the Atlantic.

I've eaten sweet papaya from a low hanging tree in Tahiti.

I've glimpsed Paradise.

Life made sense when I was all at sea.

8

'It will be soon,' whispers Nobody.

'Summer is nearly over and still no yard,' I say. Half a year done.

'I'll tell you all then – we'll be on our way. Save your strength.'

But I can't lie here. The night nips at me. There's light in the passage, someone drifts out there.

I stand up. Shake life into my arms, rub blood into my head, scratch my back.

I step over Old Man Hooke lying dead still. My foot catches in the air. I reach down, the lace stretched tight behind me. Old Man Hooke has hold of it, his teeth biting down hard. He lets go. I crouch next to him.

'They've taken my body,' he says. 'Left only my head. You?'

'Taking first watch.' I turn to look at the door.

Old Man Hooke says, 'I heard you muttering in your sleep.'

Good that he should think that, he's an old man, don't want him to worry and poke about in my plans. I mean for them to sign me out but a marine must always be prepared for anything. Old Man Hooke nudges my boot with his head.

He says, 'Every man must have something to get him through the darkest times. Can I ask?'

'The debt I mean to collect.'

'The past will only drag you under,' he says. 'No, don't listen to me, an old fool. The past keeps me.' He nudges me again. 'I carry it about my neck. Reach down in the straw.'

I feel the heat from his chest, skin beneath my hand, and something else. A piece of leather braid. I lift it up.

The light from the passage flickers on a coin. Old Man Hooke chuckles. 'That's the first thing my wife gave me. We weren't married then of course. She came to my father's haberdashery. I promised her on our wedding night I'd wear this coin always, made her promise to see me buried with it, even made the keepers promise it.'

I lay the guinea back down.

'There must be someone for you, James.'

'Love never did me no good.'

I leave his head to sleep. Take a pace of the room. But my skin itches, deep between my shoulders. I rub my back on the wall, on the door. Snores, coughs, the cries of other men – let these things drown out Hooke's tale of his wife.

Once my father told me about how he met my mother in a town called Farnham back in England. She was buying carrots at the market, a wide row of stalls that ran up the hill, the town's main street. At the top of that hill was a castle. When my mother straightened up from checking the wares, the keep in the distance lined up with her head, like a crown.

My skin is scarred by love: an English rose on my arm for my mother, a star on my chest...

The itch won't shift. Only it is more than that – a crawling through the flesh like weevils in biscuit – wriggling, churning, surfacing. It snakes between my ribs, from my back to my chest. I lift my shirt, see the letters appear one by one: *R-u-t-h*. She's tattooed on me, ink leaking, slithering over me. Her name stained into my skin – *Ruth* – the weight I can't quite bear.

Burning up my neck, scorching my cheek.

Sweet pea, sweetheart, sweet siren.

Ink in my mouth. Spluttering. Bubbling between my teeth. Staining my lips. Dribbling down my chin.

I'm puking black ink. I'm puking up her name, spitting into the darkness, 'Ruth.'

Tear open my shirt. The black letters bleed into the star on my chest, darkening it like a cloud across the sky.

*

'Mothers nursing,' I tell Fletcher. 'Children sleeping at their parent's feet. Men and women, families all together.'

Fletcher asks the same question each time, 'How did you see from the deck?'

The Samoan sharpens his hammer, mixes ash into ink. He throws the bones of his fish supper into the fire. He's not listening to us.

'Reefs,' I say. 'Channels close to shore were deepest. Fires. They watched all of life in there, had no interest in passing ships.'

The Samoan pats the bale. 'Soa,' he says.

I lie down, tufts of hay prickle through my trousers.

Fletcher touches the bloody four pointed star on his chest. 'I checked on Bligh's charts. A point of the star for each close island. Trust me, this is the way.'

'You're the sailor.'

'We're all voyagers through this life,' Fletcher says.

'A map to Paradise.' I take the bottle of rum he offers, bite the cork. The last spicy trace warms my mouth.

As the needle pierces my skin and the colour runs into me, I feel an uplifting of joy, just as Fletcher must have done only moments before. I imagine it is close to the ecstasy of saints my father told me about as a boy.

The needle strikes again, vibrating with the blow from a small hammer. I let out a cry.

Fletcher says, 'Shall he stop?'

I shake my head. A wave of cool relief as the Samoan dabs at the blood and ink, wiping me clean.

The hammer falls again and again, and the pain comes again and again. And just when I can take no more – the four pointed star is done. All complete.

9

Frosts melted to mud then dried to dust and now dampened, by autumn rain, it turns to mud again as we march in the yard. Nine months have passed since they locked me up. Outside at last. No man wears a blanket, no sign of Nobody in the yard. What if there's a different yard? What if he's changed his mind? The sun hits the back wall. I could shut my eyes, see myself on board again. I miss the burn of rum. But I don't want to miss Nobody.

I take another turn in the yard. Starboard is a gate, not the one we came in by; perhaps more men might come from there. Fleet stands by the gateposts, smoking his pipe. I miss the heat of tobacco. Fleet rubs the buttons of a new leather waistcoat; he likes to take the best from the new ones.

Rodley enters the yard from the starboard gate, jingling the keys tied to his belt. Fleet waves him through. He's bringing more crew out, huddled together. Do any of them have a blanket? Rodley pokes a man with his stick, guides him over to Fleet. Parrot Boy is chasing a feather in the air, he blocks my sight of the new arrivals. The keepers and the man stand by the gate. The new crew drift into the yard, but they're too clumped together. Is that a blanket, deep in the midst of them?

Fleet flicks Rodley's new collar. 'Dressing like Haslam don't make you like Haslam.'

Rodley shrugs him off. He would be a pretty boy but for a squint makes him look angry all the time. As if he senses me staring he turns about. Rodley points my way with the tip of his stick.

The doorway behind me is locked. There are bricks on all sides; the windows, high up in the walls, are thin as slits. I've worn breeches would give a man more room to move. But I can't leave without finding Nobody.

The keepers stand close, shoulders raised against the sharp wind that runs along the walls like cornered rats.

Old Man Hooke hops towards me. 'You're wise to keep an eye on them.'

His gown flaps, tangling us together. He doesn't want to be caught chatting out here. No fair weather trips out to the yard like he said – what else has he got wrong. I won't wait a year to find there is no out. A year to be weakened, a year to catch the madness which sickens every living thing in this place – a year could do for me. I must find the man in the blanket.

Hooke puts his hand to his nose, muffling his voice. 'They've brought a cellar dweller with them.'

'Cellar?' I try to step around him, get a better look at the new arrivals, but Parrot Boy bumps into me, pushing me back. His dark hair grown long again.

'Where they send those can't or won't make it to the bucket. That man with the keepers, he's from down there. But not of that sort.' He lifts his hand to whisper, 'He's terrified to pass water.'

I haven't met his sort yet. I've met those missing bits of themselves, those imagining themselves to be others, those too far gone to know, but a man who is afraid to give something away? He don't look the sort, could pass as a keeper. He looks like he's tasted meat this week – red-cheeked, head straight, mouth open. I wonder how he does it. If he just hates pissing, or if he makes his body a bucket? But it's a man in a blanket I want.

'He's a soldier,' Old Man Hooke says, 'can tell by the wide stance.'

The new crew start to float apart. A streak of daylight points the way. A man walks with a blanket about his shoulders, lifts it over his head.

Nobody.

He shuffles, keeping close to the wall. Thin legs, a curve to his back as if he feels the pinch of winter coming for him. I walk towards Nobody – has to be him. I step around the soldier, move swiftly past the keepers, call out, 'Hoa there!'

Nobody has the blanket bunched tight under his chin, hiding his face, but he lifts his head. I'm not one who considers himself remarkable enough to be remembered so I take no offence that he doesn't call back. When I'm close enough I'll tell him who I am. Clouds gather – it will piss on us all.

Fleet calls out, 'You, marine. Get back here.'

I'm nearly at the blanket; if I can just reach it then he will know me. I've given the keepers no trouble, not in the time I've been here. Not through those first winter months when blood flowed like mud, and not when the sharp stink of the spring Thames tide came, and not when clouds parted and the white heat of the sun was exposed.

Fleet stomps up behind me, bringing the cold creep of winter against my back. He puts a hand on my shoulder.

I'm too far from a wall to let the bricks swallow me up, or crawl into the crevices and joints of this place, which shouldn't be called a hospital but what it really is – a prison.

I must get out, must set sail, must hunt Fletcher, must finish him.

The other crew have stepped back. I'm out here blowing around like a topgallant sail in a squall.

Fleet drags me back. 'We're here to keep order,' he says. Keeper of many things but not order, I think to myself but don't say. He spins me about. 'What do you think, Rodley?'

Rodley paces. He's making a show of that stick, taking the moment as his. He prods the soldier towards me. I've not seen his face before, although in the months I've been here I've had time to learn the faces of those around. There's only one I want to see: Nobody. I have to hear his plan. Have to know there is more than one way out.

Rodley raises the staff, measures me against it. I know I come up short next to the soldier. Others have made such an error.

Fleet sighs. 'Do you take the wager or not, Rodley?'

The soldier's jaw is wider than his brow. He's taller than me and I'm not a small man. He's broader than me and I'm built to last months at sea. His arms swing as he paces, broad palms scooping the air – ha, his hands are small. My wrists – that's where I've the advantage on him. I make fists behind my back. My wrists are wide as my arms, thick like posts. But he's not the one I'm here to see.

Rodley, sly as ever, grins. 'I'll take the wager.'

Nobody in his blanket shifts about, he looks over. How will he know me?

'Set to it.' Rodley bangs the stick in the mud.

Fleet kicks it away. 'You'll be buying me new breeches if you ruin these.'

Fleet's in low down dirty trousers, any fool can see that. This world is full of blind madness. But it isn't my place to make them see that. I could wave at Nobody, shout out, but our business isn't for all to know. The soldier's hands cradle his gut, he doesn't listen to the keepers but holds ground a step behind them.

The keepers have some foolishness planned for that soldier and me. I've not got time to waste. I let my eyes lose their gaze; my head dips on my shoulder, like I've seen the old types slumped on straw in the cell. Even Rodley blinks. 'Well, not today. Haslam's about this morning. Another day?'

I stare at Nobody, will him to look over at me. Let me be seen.

Fleet laughs. 'Haslam and that book. Thinks he'll get hisself accepted into the parlours of the rich and good. Haslam ain't going to be about before he's tucked away some buns and sweet coffee.' Fleet slaps the soldier's neck like they're old mates. 'Raise your fists.'

The crew won't look at me, not even Old Man Hooke. They've turned their backs like I'm an anchor ready to be dropped in the waves. They're afraid I'll drag them under. The soldier bounces on his heels – springy bugger. His well-fed cheeks and thick muscles make the rest of us look like flat ink figures. Dried beef, or bone soup, hot pease, hardtack boiled with oatmeal, I even miss that. I wish there was a bell in here to mark the hours – surely another has passed since they took watch in front of me.

'If he don't fight – that's a win for my soldier,' Fleet adds.

Rodley prods the staff into my gut. 'He'll fight.'

I hold myself still. Look up, Nobody. Look up!

The soldier laughs... I wish he hadn't.

I'm holding myself in, pressing my fists deeper into my back.

Something moves in the mud at my feet. An eye. Gills. A mackerel lifts its head. What is it doing there? The mackerel stands on its tail, but it moves nowhere, or seems not to, so slowly does it sway. A green glint to its scales that dulls, as I watch, like it's dying down there. I'm not the only one to see it: Nobody stumbles forward, he's behind the keepers. They're too intent on their fun, don't notice him. And for a moment the blanket lifts, caught by the breeze.

That face.

Not nobody.

The high forehead, the dark brows, the dark eyes. And poking up from his open shirt, the point of a star tattoo on his chest. I would know that man anywhere, he hasn't changed, he never will: Fletcher Christian.

I shout out, 'I'm coming for you.'

The soldier throws a bored punch. I wish he hadn't.

But now he's gone and touched me. He thinks all he need do is blow and my sails will flap, broadsided. He thinks he can capsize me. And all I want is that blanket-wearing, traitorous bastard – Fletcher.

Nothing will keep my hands from Fletcher's throat. They're shouting at me – too far away to hear.

I rush forward, crushing the mackerel into the muck. Hands thrust me back. They all think I'm a coward, for letting Fletcher get away the first time. The soldier trots around me, giving a good show. What sort of man gets too scared to piss? Perhaps he thinks he'll drown the world. I'll drown them all if they keep me from my justice. Fletcher tries to cover his face with the blanket – no hiding from me now – he stumbles backwards.

The solider comes at me again. My legs shake as his fist shifts my chin up into my teeth. He hasn't noticed my wrists. I aim to his side, low.

I'll fight them all to get at Fletcher. He thought he could trick me again, laughing at me behind that wall. He makes for the gate, shuffling like an old man to disguise himself.

I punch the soldier's back once. Twice.

The soldier stares at his breeches. He can't stop it now. The dark stain spreads down to his knees, puddles at his feet.

Maybe he will drown us all.

The dirty, filthy beast. He pisses and pisses. He doesn't move. Sweat blinds him. He's leaking all over like an old cockboat. Stinking dog, to do that where men can see him. I smash into him with my shoulders. He falls backwards onto his knees. Not fit to be seen. Down to the cellar with you.

I'll fight the man I want – Fletcher Christian. 'I'll kill you.'

My wrists are posts to batter my way to Fletcher. I'll make him eat that blanket before I finish him.

Down, down goes the soldier. His cheek shatters like a snapped chicken bone.

I'm strong as a giant. I could break through these walls with my shoulders. I could leap the roof with one bound. I could pound this place into the mud with my fists. I kick the soldier out of my way. He shames himself.

I'm nearly at the gate. Fletcher Christian won't get away from me this time. I snatch at the grey blanket.

Fleet grabs Rodley's stick, lifts it high in the air.

All goes black. I am blackness.

10

I'm down in the murk, crushed like that mackerel. If I hold still, whatever swims around me may slip by. A splashing sound. Closer now. Something brushes against my sole. I give a warning kick. It slithers up my leg. When it reaches the back of my knee, I know what caresses me.

I hiss, 'Get away, bitch.'

Ruth's lips flutter against my skin. 'You've been calling.'

I keep my eyes closed. Ruth breathes on me, the thin skin there grows hot.

'I've been inside,' she whispers.

'Inside is beautiful.' The words are out before I can stop them.

'You remember.' Her hair falls against my back, her hands slide over my shoulders. 'We'll stay there together, won't we, James?'

Her chin presses into the side of my neck.

Don't open your eyes, you fool.

She kisses my cheek.

'Get fu –' She presses a finger to my lips, silences me. I feel the bone, the warmth. That green smell: rosemary, salt, grass.

She whispers, 'We can be together – if you try...'

Her bare feet, cold as usual, tread in against the back of my legs. Her knees on my buttocks. 'Inside is our hiding place. No one will find us there.'

Only there is a cold wind blowing. There's grit and an itching. I'm going to open my eyes, I know I am. I'm going to lose again, and again, just as I always lose.

I open my eyes...

Back in the graveyard at Portsmouth. Sea mist thickens to drizzle; it shines on Ruth's dark hair. *I wish this was a dream, I wish I was deep asleep*. Ruth turns when I call her name. *Sweet pea, sweetheart...*

'Ruth, I've been looking for you.'

The Royal Garrison Church looms behind her, silhouetted in the thickening mist. She turns her face towards me, her body still pointed to the church. 'I prayed for it, James Norris. They told me your ship was sunk.' She pulls a grey blanket tight about herself.

'Didn't I tell you I'd be back? What a waste of prayers.'

Out on the water winter sun breaks through the clouds, drops of light sparkling. She smiles. 'I prayed so hard and you didn't come. But that's your religion – out there.' She nods, brushes down her skirts, like she'd been the one to summon me home across the seas.

I laugh. 'I expected you at the dock. It was the girls told me you'd be here, not God.'

I can't wait any longer: months, months, months of waking with wood, her face, her breasts, her buttocks melting away from me in daylight. Now I need to fill my hands with Ruth again.

'Don't I even get a kiss?' I step forward, twist her about, lift her up in my arms.

Her skirts swing, she steadies her hands on my hips. She is between me and the sea, the sky; the tight blue bodice, its worn threads are soft to the touch. I slide my cheek against her breasts. But there is a heaviness to her, pulling her down. She drops lower until her feet are back in the mud. My hands slip down her back, gathering the wool of her skirts, kneading her buttocks.

'Careful,' she whispers.

'Dead don't care what we do, and no one else is about.'

This isn't the welcome I expected. She leans away from me like a sapling bending in the wind. 'If you want to fuck a whore go back to the docks.' Her words slap against me. 'If you want me...' She reaches out for my hand.

Her dress is stretched tight. The blanket around her shoulders slips, her stomach pushing out in front. The drizzle lightens like held back tears, the stray drops falling on our heads.

Her hands twitch to that lump, cradling it with her linked fingers. 'Yours,' she says.

She takes a step towards me, leans in. She kisses me. Her arms swing loose like sails ready for the folding.

I catch hold of them, thrust her back to make sure. She's caught against a tombstone, can't go any further. There's life inside her. 'When?'

'Soon.' She doesn't try to pull away. 'I know a woman will give us a room. There's plenty of work at the docks. And –'

I squeeze her arms. 'I've been at sea seventeen months.'

'Happens sometimes, babies don't be ready to come out.'

She kisses me again. The lie burns my lips raw.

I haul her towards me, my head drops to her shoulder. She twists her fingers into my hair. She sighs, the air runs out of her and I want her to not breathe in again, for her body to deflate, for her to be what she was. I want her. Her damp hair scratches against my mouth but it can't hold back my voice.

'Whore.'

She twists like a landed fish in my hands. 'Not with you.'

I feel the slime, the scales, the stink. I push her away. 'Didn't I always pay my way?'

'He who has no faults is not born.' The sun shines behind her, but it is far out at sea; that warmth will be too late to reach us.

The leaves start to dance, a trade wind is brewing. I know it carries something cruel and ugly. Something is going to happen and it will happen because of me.

I need to know *his* name. 'Who done it?'

Ruth shakes her head. 'I only ever wanted you inside me.'

She's making a fool of me. Laughter bubbles up from the sea. I turn. Two drunken sailors stagger against the wall. Slump over it, watching me.

I point. 'Is it one of them?'

She stares up at me. 'He told me you weren't coming back.'

'Who?'

'Fletcher.'

She wants to hurt me. Fletcher and me have great plans, we're after Paradise. He wouldn't do what she says. He's my brother – like a brother. But we haven't been on the same ship this last voyage.... Fletcher's been back in Portsmouth for how long? I grip her chin, force her to look. 'Liar!'

She seems to come awake at that. Snaps with her teeth, flicks her head back. 'I want this baby to be yours. And there was a son. Our son –'

'Lying whore.' I wipe my hand on my shirt, I want the smell of her off me.

'Our son couldn't hold on for your return. He slipped out of me –'

I slap the lie out of her mouth. But she doesn't stop,

'Down on the shore... out into the sea.'

I squeeze my hands into fists, and she sees. She pushes me in the chest. She steps in so close, the pink of her tongue flashes in her mouth. 'Our boy came out with a rope about his neck – probably how any son of yours would end his days.'

I raise my fist. She grabs it, presses it to her face, kisses my knuckles. 'I'll raise this child as ours.'

'I'll not give it my name.'

Her head sinks, she stumbles back, sitting down hard on top a gravestone. She deflates like a dropped sail, face white as the stone.

'You're a bloody fool, James Norris.' She hits out, palms against my chest, forcing me off balance. 'Why won't you let us be happy?'

One of the drunks pisses against the wall. He whistles for attention. 'That's it, lad. Don't give her a guinea. She's probably done half the fleet over with that sad tale.'

His friend laughs but covers his mouth with his fist when Ruth picks up a stone, hurls it at them. Her aim is good. He collects his mate, they stagger away. The pisser laughing, the other snorting as he holds up his mate.

I wish I was that soaked in rum.

I wish that some other sod was standing here in my place. Not Fletcher. No, not him.

'Do you know why I'm here?' Ruth pulls a corn dolly out of her dress. It is no bigger than a plum. 'I made a cross with his name. I remembered the letters you taught me.'

She holds it up to my face. My initials are burned on the corn. I feel a rope about my neck – yanked tight.

The sailors sing, voices drifting over the headstones, 'The maid I left behind me.'

Ruth puts her hand out, it settles on my chest like the leaves blowing against the low stone wall of the graveyard. 'You are my starlight, James Norris.' She reaches for the star tattoo on my chest.

I step away, won't give her the answer she wants.

She waits, lips parted, arms open. 'Cariad...'

I want to push her face into the mud, kick that lump inside her. I shove past her, have to be away before I finish her.

Her voice lifts and trails after me. 'Huryl fawr.'

I stop, lunge back, grabbing her hands. The cunning bitch smiles, thinks we're going to embrace. I snatch the corn dolly from her. Crush it. Stamp it into the mud. Spit on it.

She's too stonehearted to even cry.

11

I wake, in my bed at the Mission, with a drowsy head, the sort of waking when you think for a moment you're still swaying in your hammock. A sliver of light slices the berth in half. So, not a rich man with a fresh painted carriage and strong-legged horse, not cuddled up to a lass with tits as springy as fresh baked bread. Oh well, good or bad, a dream is a dream, on with the morning.

Something holds me down. Pins nick my scalp, something sits heavy on my crown. Can't move. I try to turn my head.

Not the Mission, not the graveyard, but a place even further from life.

The keepers have hold of my arms, pressing me down into the straw. The surgeon removes a measuring instrument off my head as though he was plotting a course over the Atlantic on me.

'Pity! It won't be today,' he says. 'I've yet to add an American to my collection.'

Fleet peers at me. 'Don't look no different from an Englishman.'

'Don't sound it neither,' Rodley says.

Fleet says, 'Too long at sea.'

The surgeon blows his nose on an embroidered handkerchief. He takes his instruments, folds them up in a black leather case.

He leaves behind the sharp stink of gin – I could cut myself open on it if I'm not careful. The keepers follow him from the room.

I rub the split at the back of my head, matted with blood and hair. How long have I been asleep? Long enough for mice to have carried off the straw beneath me, and moths to have eaten through my shirt. I slept, I know I did, but not sea air or rum sleep. An emptying is what it was, carved out like a piece of scrimshaw. I had my hands on him, Fletcher Christian, and yet he lives.

Old Man Hooke kneels beside me. He smiles, 'Only my lower legs missing.' He lifts my head, holds a cup to my lips.

I drink and drink.

Still in the same room, still the same crew. Ha! Not incurable yet, or maybe they'll hold it against me like St Peter at the gates when my day comes – they'll read a list of my sins and send me down for all eternity.

Old Man Hooke starts to shuffle toward the water bucket.

I hold him back. 'How long?'

'Days.'

Three months less a day or two, is all I have left. But what waits for me out there? I cough, rub my throat. Old Man Hooke helps me sit up against the wall.

'I hear the soldier still hasn't woken,' he says.

'No man in this place is awake.' I lay my hand on the bricks. 'So, the surgeon wants to carve me like a hog, the keepers want me for their own dancing bear. And Fletcher Christian means to drive me mad.'

'Fletcher Christian?'

I draw him close, whisper, 'Where better for a mutineer, a treacherous beast to hide than amongst fools? He'll have planned it all with that sly brother of his. But he wasn't expecting me!' I pick at the dry skin on my lips.

Some luck's come my way at last. I was planning on sailing after him, hunting him through paradise to push him through the gates of hell. Now all I have to do is get through that wall.

Old Man Hooke shakes his head. 'It can't be.'

'I was lunatic for a moment perhaps.' I bang my fist against the wall. 'But I'm not one.'

He sighs. 'Men change, faces change –'

'I saw the star.' I tug open my shirt, show him the same tattoo on my chest. 'You ever been to Paradise?'

'There's happiness in this life, James, but Paradise is for the next –'

'I've seen it.' I place my hand on my heart. 'This star is my map.'

'Then follow it. A few months, and you can set sail again.'

'Spring is the best time to make a running…' I shake my head. 'How can I go there when the devil still walks beside me?' I hit the wall with my knuckles.

'I'll fetch you more water.' He crawls off to the bucket by the door.

I punch the wall again; a pile of dust and mortar lies beneath my fist. 'I know you're there.'

'Let me sleep. The yard – that was your chance, man. There'll not be another.'

'I know you.'

'I'm Nobody.'

'But I know who Nobody is.'

'Tell me.'

I whisper, 'If I say your name out loud they'll hang you.'

'What did I do?'

I laugh. 'You never used to be this funny.' But that's a lie; I agreed with him once on some odd or sod and he said, 'Everyone knows when England eats beans, America farts.' I nearly spouted beer out my nose. Well, he'll not find me falling in with him now.

He says, 'They call me Nobody and I know nothing of my life before this room.'

'Always were good at playing the innocent.' Now, that is true.

'I hoped it wasn't so but why else would they lock me up. I am bad.'

'Damn fucking right.'

'You must be bad too. I shan't listen to you.'

'I'll be the voice in the wall,' I say. 'I'll not let you sleep, not let you forget.'

I punch the hole, it crumbles more. Punch. Punch.

He whispers, 'They're signing me over to the incurables by the end of the week. I heard so from the keepers.'

I crush the straw in my fist. I must be the one to push him through those gates to hell.

'Don't let them take me,' he says.

'I'm coming, that I promise.'

'Then I think you must be a friend.'

I roll away from the wall, try to pull my shirt over my ears. If he's sent to the cellar or some other hole and hid from me again, is it punishment enough? Can I sail away knowing he's suffering but alive? I sit up, press my head between my knees. He's full of poison. It drips down inside me.

Old Man Hooke is back, places the cup beside me. 'You're bleeding,' he says, tearing a piece of his gown, holding it out to me.

I suck my knuckles, tuck the cloth about them. 'Snivelling wretch couldn't even stand his ownself in paradise, that's why he's back.'

Hooke lifts my hand, tightens the wrapping. 'Those cuts won't heal,' he says. 'If they were just cuts I don't suppose it would matter. But they never are.' He shakes his head. 'Be careful, this place can show a man what he wants to see.'

'I know it was Fletcher. He is here, I feel it.'

I've seen things after eating bad beef, after taking too much grog like that one time a lascar boy clawed his way out of my chest, a jagged seashell for a mouth.

No, it's not that.

'Hooke, I have to get into that room.'

'Our time here is nearly done.'

'I've a debt I must collect from that traitor. I'll go mad if I can't.'

'There's no leaving this place with blood on your hands.'

'I could rid myself of all of it, if you'd only help me get a key from the keepers,' I say.

'There's no leaving madness behind in this place.'

The keepers are wild as dogs, but even dogs can be made to chase their own tails. I could get to Fletcher in that room and be back before they even noticed. Who'd care about one more dead soul in this place?

'Thought we were ma –' I shove him away. 'Forget it. I'll do it on my own.'

'Son, please.'

'I'm not that, be grateful for it.'

'My tongue brings me no end of trouble. But I'll help you all I can.'

I want to thank him, want to say he's a true friend – only

there's no believing in such things now. I pat his shoulder, push some more straw his way. 'Rest yourself,' I say, turning to face the wall.

Fletcher Christian thought never to see me again. Now here I am – his nightmare. It was black as hell that last night we met. A storm blanketed the whole city of Portsmouth, the docks hidden under the downpour – a man could hold out his hand and think the world beyond disappeared, so black was that night.

But I can see that night at any time, it has never left me...

*

A splattering of raindrops hit the flagstone floor. I slap my hat again, hard against my leg. There's no getting dry. The Dolphin steams, fogged with smoke. The wood panels dark as blood.

I've come here because this is where I always come.

I need safe harbour after parting with Ruth. Damn her. I kick the door shut. The wind bangs the shutters, gutters the fires, and no one turns to stare at a half-drowned man. My legs shake and I've not even a drink inside me yet. I lean against the wooden walls, slide deeper inside. I need ballast to steady me – beer, rum.

The panelled passage hides heads at tables, all men face the fire, seeking comfort on such a treacherous night. No tables left, nowhere to hide myself.

A hand slaps my back. 'James. Praise be, you're back.'

'Fletcher.' I keep my head lowered. My coat and hat weep around me, don't need him to see my wet face.

He puts an arm about me. 'You look as though you've been overboard again.' He guides me to the fire. 'Make room. Room there. This man needs the warmth more than you.'

The group of men, master's mates, surgeon's mates, shuffle on the benches – ranking themselves as gentlemen. They eye my patched breeches, the nails in my boots. But when Fletcher turns to me, the sympathy in his eyes near sets me to weeping.

He rubs heat into my hands, unwinds a scarf from his own neck, wraps it about me. Like the good brother he is, there aren't questions or demands. He sits beside me, drinks, waits for the beer to loosen my lips. He tells me of his own brother, Charles, a broken man, caught up in some mutiny.

I take another mouthful; it brings some summer to this winter night.

I put my hands on Fletcher's, lean in. 'She's gone, Fletcher.'

'Remind me.' He turns to wink at the man next to him.

'Ruth.'

'Dear Lord, is that all? It's just a woman, boys. Back to your grog.' He smiles.

I grab his cup, gulp down the rest of the malty beer. He slaps me on the back. Orders two more with a shout. I reach for the purse; he pushes my hand away.

'Rum all round,' he calls. The other men on the benches lift their cups at him.

He says no more until the rum arrives. He's not one to spend his money so. No one is as they should be today. Ruth, Fletcher. No, I won't put those names together. She's a liar. Like a dead limb at sea, it has to be sawn off and cauterised, the only way to save a man's life.

I raise the tot of rum to Fletcher. 'Fair winds and following seas.'

'I'll soon have no need for money – she's only ever run out on me.'

I sit up. Fletcher nods. We spoke of it often before, the land where no money was needed. Seashells, breadfruit, livestock – these were the treasures of that place. I'd told Fletcher of its many jewels.

Fletcher holds a finger to his lips, shakes his head. 'Don't name it, not yet.' He takes another drop, wipes his clammy mouth on his sleeve. 'My only fear was you'd not be back in time.'

'Were there rumours I was sunk?'

He laughs, shakes his head. 'I've seen you in the water, you float.' He pats me on the back, addresses the bench. 'This man here saved my life.'

There are nods and groans. The others go back to their chatter about dogs, horses, and fine ladies.

He laughs again. 'See, I've bored the crew with tales of my great friend – No –' he shakes his head, rubs his chest over the hidden tattoo '– my brother James Norris. More rum!'

And more is brought, and more is drunk.

He puts a hand on the back of my neck, hauls me forward. Our foreheads touch. He whispers, 'For all we've dreamed.' He raises his eyebrows, mouths the word, *Paradise*. 'You promised me, James. Always knew you were telling me the truth.'

He lets go, sits back, the bench rocks. It's all we've spoken of for years, since the night he clung to me in the Atlantic Ocean, the years together on Cambridge and Eurydice, the years' meeting on docks, in pubs. Paradise.

He grins. 'You'll not guess what the ship's called.'

He's playing like a boy with a new toy soldier, and I want to laugh but the sourness of earlier in the graveyard, with Ruth, still curdles everything. Why would she say Fletcher? To hurt me is all. Yes, that can be the only reason.

Fletcher shakes my arm. 'She's called Bounty. What perfect omen is that?'

I need more grog, more heat from the fire to keep up with Fletcher. His cheeks burn red; he taps his knuckles on his knee. He rolls his bottom lip back and forth against his upper teeth. He crackles just as much as the fire.

'She's a blunt nosed little ship but –'

One of the men calls over. 'Bligh can't sail his way to the Channel I heard.'

Fletcher rubs his forehead. 'It's this storm!' He turns to me. 'We can't speak here. Come with me to the Bounty.'

'I go where they send me.'

'Old Bligh, he's master and commander. The surgeon's mate signed on as an able seaman. Bligh will get you assigned, if we ask. Trust me.'

And I do trust him. Like brothers. Hats on, coats on, we head into the night.

Rain lashes sharp as a cat o' nine tails. I saved his life. Tried to catch him when he fell from the rigging. Followed him into the ocean. Held him afloat. Brothers.

It happens sometimes, babies don't be ready to come out.

I wrap the scarf he gave me tighter against the storm. Enough water to wash the salt from the sea. It beats against us. Fletcher stumbles, links his arm through mine. We keep close or risk being swept apart. All sensible souls are tucked up by fires, under blankets. I wonder where Ruth lies. No, that's no care of mine.

He who has no faults is not born.

I shout to be heard. 'Don't care where the Bounty sails. Sign me up. A man rots on land.'

Fletcher waves me into the shelter of a chandler's porch. The shop is closed but candlelight drips from an upstairs window.

'Don't care?' He pulls at the buttons of his jacket, tears at the shirt, slaps his hand on the star. 'What's this?'

I rub rain from my face. 'A map to paradise.'

'Say it like it means something.' He laughs. 'But I forget – there are more important things like your broken cock.'

He told me you weren't coming back.

Fletcher lays his hands on my shoulders, presses his forehead to mine. 'All that's the past. This is our future, all we've spoke of – out there... And you're downhearted over some girl –'

'Ruth was always more than that, Fletcher.' The graveyard, the mud, the corn dolly – I've no words for any of those things. It's like she slit me open, slopped my guts to the dogs.

'No, I'm sorry, not some girl – some whore.'

I grab his arm. 'Don't say that.'

'We're off to Paradise. Nothing should stand in the way of that.' He tries to pull me onwards. 'Not my brothers, my mother. I'm giving up everything.'

I lean against the door, need to keep dry for a moment longer. 'I've nothing to give up now.'

'That's a blessing, you're not a man to give up – she was causing you to drift. She wasn't worth –'

'What did you do, Fletcher?'

He half turns. 'What any brother would! Saved you.'

'From Ruth?'

Fletcher stands in the rain, seems not to notice. 'You couldn't see what she was. And you would have stayed with her, given up on Paradise.' Fletcher throws back his head as if he feels sunshine on his face.

'She was going to ruin it,' I say stepping out into the rain, boot to boot with Fletcher. 'So you ruined her?'

He rubs his fingers over the star. 'She didn't even care enough to wait and see if you returned. I turned her away for weeks. But you had to know what she was.'

Ruth didn't even care if I was dead... went straight on to the next – replaced as quickly as my father replaced my mother with another wife – I was never loved.

'You were going to break your promise, James, for a whor –'

I thrust my hands about his neck. 'Don't say it.'

Fletcher tries to bat my hands away. There's no breaking my grip. He squeezes his fingers between my hand and his skin. 'James – did it for you...'

'You just wanted what I had.' I squeeze tighter.

'Brothers mean more than anything.' Rain fills his open mouth.

I nearly have him to his knees. 'You've taken everything.'

He claws at me, snatches at the scarf he earlier wrapped about my neck. Off balance, we fall into the mud. The scarf unravels.

A voice shouts, 'What's occurring? Foul enough night as it is.'

I'm lifted off Fletcher, thrown to the ground. I roll over, rub my neck. Rain soaks into my shirt and breeches. Fletcher is already up on his feet, bouncing on his heels, shaking hands with the two men in long coats and wide brimmed hats. First Mates, I'm sure of it.

One says, 'Bligh sent us. We're putting off to the Isle of Wight. You'd best get back. We'll see to this?'

Fletcher shakes his head. 'A disagreement –'

'Does Bligh know you're about with lowdown sorts?'

The other says, 'What's he doing with your scarf?'

Fletcher snatches the scarf, my head bangs back on the

cobbles. He bends over, whispers, 'You're a mad fool, James Norris.' He prods me with his boot as if I'm some shit he can scrape off. 'When you come to your senses you know where to find me.' He touches his fingers to my chest, to the hidden star.

Fletcher puts on his best voice. 'He's trying to tell me some tale about why he needed the scarf, says he's too scared to set to sea again for an honest penny.'

'Too much a coward to sail,' says one.

'Needs a lesson,' says the other.

Fletcher walks into the dark rain, he disappears.

The two sailors come at me. I get in some hits. I take all that they give. Bloodied nose, bruised body, smashed hands. Give more, I want to shout, for being a fool, for trusting Fletcher, for loving Ruth – give me more to take away that pain. Only I can't shout, my mouth brims with blood.

I lie still.

A light moves over me, a warm breath. My eyes swollen shut.

Why couldn't you let us be happy, James?

By the time I finally heave myself up, puking into the mud, Bounty has sailed. I stand on the dock, spit blood into the harbour waves – cursing the day I ever met Fletcher Christian.

12

Maybe I am what they say I am.

I was never a good man.

No, that can't be true.

I have been happy.

I have felt rain fall heavy on me.

I have been loved.

I have often felt far from everyone.

13

I'm the first awake. I let Old Man Hooke rest a little longer, walking the tumbled rows of still sleeping men and spilled straw, calling as I go, 'Show a leg.'

The stink of the shit bucket burns me. I stand by the window, catch the cold draught and swallow it down. Parrot Boy flutters about the room, getting too close to Old Man Hooke, close enough to trample him. I rush over. Parrot Boy stares at me with those black eyes, opens his mouth but no sound comes out.

'Get away from him,' I say. 'Go on, find another perch.'

But Old Man Hooke hasn't moved. He lies on his back, arms and legs trembling in the morning light. I stare down at him. His arms twitch.

'Oh, this is good,' I say. 'You've the start on me, Old Man Hooke.'

True to his word, the fellow is a friend after all. The key is mine. I pinch my leg to hold back the laughter. I call out, 'Keeper!'

More men wake, joining in the call.

I lift Old Man Hooke's head. 'Don't play it too hard,' I say. 'They'll smell a rat. Just need enough time to get the key.'

I place his head on my knee, a loosening in his fingers and jaw. I undo the last button on his gown. He still shakes.

'Lie still now, they'll take a moment,' I say, rubbing my hand over the sharp stubble on his head, sweeping off the loose straw.

The crew crowd around, watching Hooke but also watching me. I want to leap up, run to the door, burst through it as the keepers arrive. Old Man Hooke grabs my hand, he steadies me. Rodley opens the door, keys rattling. The surgeon follows him in. Rodley kicks at men still lying on the floor, rolling them aside. 'Over here, Surgeon Crowther.'

I hold my place.

'Back now, you men.' The surgeon flaps his hands, the crew step away.

Crowther's stench of gin and piss would be enough to revive most men but not Hooke – he holds steady.

'Hurry now. I need to bleed this man.' Crowther shoves his bag into Rodley's arms.

Crowther's greasy strands of hair stick to his scalp. He keeps touching his forehead as if he's still wearing his wig. Rodley grins, places the bag carefully on the floor, paying it more care than Hooke. Crowther waits with his hands out; they shake being so far from a drink. Hooke shakes too. And it strikes me he can't be much more than fifty. Ten more years, and this could be me. Bad luck Crowther should be passing the room. I've no doubt he'll do Hooke a little damage but no worse than Hooke does to himself. Once they're all at it, I have only to slip away and do what must be done – finish Fletcher Christian.

I wish Crowther clear vision and sound hands. He wipes water from the red folds under his eyes, nearly blinds himself with his own thumb. I've seen many a sailor climb the rigging in a haze of drunkenness as if their body has a memory of its own that can't be touched by drink.

I lean over to whisper, 'Keep a true course, Hooke. Won't hurt a bit.'

Crowther holds the blade like a quill, delicately balanced. What's a few gins before breakfast to such a regular as him? Some of the crew have rolled back over into sleep, others peer and chatter such things that no man would want to hear so near the end. But this is just for sport, for the key. Hooke's doing this for me.

I let Old Man Hooke's head rest on the floor. Stand up. No one looks at me.

Crowther groans, lowers himself to his knees on the other side of Hooke. He takes a deep breath, presses his thumb to each red nostril, gives a brisk snort. He lifts the knife. The rusty blade sinks into Hooke's arm. Not a sound from the old man.

Rodley has the keys on his belt. I stand close behind him, reaching around. The keys are tied with string. The knot gives easily. The metal is warm in my hand.

Old Man Hooke's tongue bulges past his lips, foam speckles his mouth, bubbles over his chin. That's not right.

Crowther's leaning too far over. He slips forward, closer than he wants to be to the stink of a lunatic. He jerks his hand. Swings back the blade.

Blood spouts, hits the back wall, trailing a red arc. He's cut Hooke deep, blood spraying from his arm. Too deep. Crowther draws out a handkerchief from the bag, wipes his face clean. Nearly at the door. I turn and even from halfway across the room, I see the slice is deep.

Still Old Man Hooke doesn't wake. No, that's not right.

'Skin is too thin,' Crowther spits at Rodley. 'Only a fool would have such thin skin.'

Rodley prods Hooke in the ribs. 'Hooke you dolt, what have you done to your skin?'

'I can't work with thin skin,' says Crowther with a shake of his head. He struggles to his feet, swaying with the knife in his hand. The crew clear a space around him.

Hooke pouts like a fish. There's no air getting into him. There's no game to this.

'Can I assist?' Haslam stands in the doorway.

Crowther holds himself up by grasping the wall. 'You deal with it. Can't take a bleeding. Thin skin.'

Haslam pushes past me. 'Hold that arm,' he says to Rodley.

Rodley just stares at the blood thickening about his boots. Crowther shuffles out the door. Everyone looks down at Hooke and his spilled blood.

The door is still open. Why can't I move? Damn Hooke, I owe him nothing.

Haslam roots in his bag.

I glance at the open door. The passage is still. No footsteps. No calls.

How long before Rodley notices the keys are gone? How long before Fleet appears? How long before another of the crew beats me to it, darts through the door?

Haslam works on his own, winding the bandage. 'That should hold the graze.'

Graze? Am I the only man to see the cut is down to the bone?

Hooke is past caring how deep the wound goes. His lips are blue. Foam dries to a crust about his mouth. Haslam still tries to get a stick between Hooke's bloated lips; uncorking a blue bottle with his own teeth.

Who knows what Hooke might have lost in the night? Perhaps they really have been at him like he always said. Maybe it was his head missing, the keepers must have stole it from him, creeping quiet as cannibals in Vanuatu.

I take a step backwards. The door is just behind me.

Hooke's an old man.

Haslam doesn't need my help.

Fuck them all.

And a madness draws me to that door. It scratches at me, calling – more tempting than a dreamed up mermaid's song. But there are other important cries. No man at sea ignores the shouts of *Man overboard*. I shove back through, down on my knees beside Haslam. Stuffing the keys under my arm.

Old Man Hooke doesn't have to die, not in this place. Let me do something good for once.

'Hold his head,' Halsam says.

In the pale morning light Haslam's mistaken me for a keeper.

I cradle Hooke's head between my hands. *What have they taken from you?*

Haslam pours the bottle into Hooke's mouth. A brown liquid dribbles out past Hooke's lips, down his neck. The smell of blood and tar hangs heavy. Something else hangs from Hooke's mouth. A thin thread, darkened by the tincture.

He has tied up his tongue, wrapped the thread round and round. I dig in Hooke's mouth with my finger. Can't keep the keys clamped under my arm.

I try to call him back, 'Did you think they'd take it from you, Hooke?' *Swim. Swim. Hold onto me*.

The keys drop. Rodley spies them, grabs me about the waist, struggling to get me on the floor. The thread is still in my grip. It yanks Hooke's head up. We are attached, him and me. Haslam sees it, takes out a small knife.

Haslam says, 'Hold him still.'

Rodley wraps his arms about my neck. His collar pops open.

'The other man, fool.'

With that word Haslam makes the keeper one of us.

If keepers are fools and apothecaries are foolish, what does that make us men? No better nor worse than them – that's what. I shake myself free of Rodley's grip but he has the keys. The collar lies trampled in the straw. His mouth is open, panting, he wants to call for Fleet, call me thief. He ties the keys back to his breeches, slips the collar inside his shirt. Rodley can't say a word, of course he can't.

I have you, Hooke. Haslam lowers the knife to the thread. It's wound too tight. The blade too thick. Haslam slices into Hooke's tongue. It bleeds more than his arm.

It doesn't take long to sink Hooke.

He drowns in his own blood.

The weight in my arms lightens, but his body is harder to hold than water. He slips from my grip, drifts to the floor. The room is quiet, quiet as it can be with all those men breathing, trying to hold themselves still. A whimpering starts up in a far corner.

I stand up, look to see who weeps for himself and not for Hooke. Too many arms, too many legs, and heads – none of them belongs to Hooke. Down at my feet his body lies complete in death. See, every bit of him is there, save the spilled blood. But Hooke himself is gone.

Fleet comes barrelling through the door. He stops when he sees Haslam on his knees.

He locks the door behind him.

I push my way through the crew, up to the porthole. The yard is empty. Hooke will be the only one to leave this place today. Fletcher will have to wait.

Haslam takes off his coat, holds it away from himself – as if he's not used to blood. He walks a trail of it out of the room, off through Bedlam's passageways. It must be sloshing in his shoes. I pick the drying blood out from under my nails, rubbing my hands on the bricks.

No getting clean.

Fleet stands over Hooke's body. He bends down, rips the leather string, holds up Hooke's guinea.

'I'll buy you a drink down the Rose and Crown, Rodley,' he says.

Rodley shakes his head. 'I don't want none.'

'He can't hurt you.' Fleet laughs.

'Always said he wanted to be buried with it. Shouldn't go against the wishes of the dead.'

Fleet shakes his head. 'For a workhouse lad you're a right soft one.' He balances Hooke's guinea on his finger. 'A cursed guinea will still fetch me a night of booze, beef and titty.'

Don't fight it, is what my father said.

The men crowd Fleet, begging for tobacco. And that's how it is only moments after a death, each man feels his own needs the more.

Hooke stains us all, from the wet straw, to the muddy floor, to the hands of each man.

I did nothing to save Hooke. I did nothing to keep his last wish.

I do nothing.

I.

Do.

Nothing.

Nothing burns in my gut.

14

The keepers are gone. The crew sleep. But for now, I have other company.

Standing by the wall is King George himself. I might not have known him if he didn't have a guinea for a head, the bust side turned to me. His head is so big I'm not sure how he came through the bars of the door but he's a king and they have their ways. Perhaps he squeezed his body through and the giant guinea was forged in the room. His mouth is cast in gold, he can't speak. But he waves his hand, slaps my shoulder, as if we are deep in talk. What would I know of what a king says? His ears are gold too, so he doesn't hear me. I can speak as I please.

'Fletcher Christian did this – he took everything and gave me this – this place. Yes, hard to know what a man might risk for Paradise...'

King George rubs his hand on his heart; a gentle tinkle of medals and silver buttons speaks for him.

'That's the pain all right,' I say.

The buttons pop like corks, each one rolling off between the rows of sleeping men. The jacket flaps open like wings. There's a wound in his chest, the skin torn, full of redness. But something moves in the king's chest. I peer closer.

Old Man Hooke stands inside the cavern where a heart should be. He stands no bigger than my thumb.

'You're dead,' I say.

He calls to me, 'My guinea. Help me find it.'

I slide a finger inside. Hot, but dry like old leather. I sink deeper. Bone, flesh. Softness. Fingers sticking. Sucking me in. Past my elbow, inside. No reaching Old Man Hooke.

15

Some are released. Some are sent up to incurables. Some are sent down to the cellars. Some stay. Some die. Such is the heads or tails of everything in life. But my year is done. February has returned, Valentine's Day. I know this because Rodley is down in the yard collecting toll kisses from the women. I take one last turn of the room. My last day in Bethlem Hospital.

I've heard no more from the voice in the wall.

Let Fletcher rot with the incurables.

I'll not get myself run aground in Bedlam. Look what happened to Hooke.

Isn't this place worse than any death?

Or I could stand at the gates, wait another year to see if Fletcher is released.

And what Fleet did to Hooke.... I won't think on that.

Only, what if there is no release, even if the rest of my life is spent on the other side of these walls?

I hit the door with my fist.

A year ago today I was raving at the Seaman's Mission, pacing in the passage, tearing my shirt, waving my neckcloth, calling out, 'What should I do?' For I remember that I despaired of getting a berth out to Tahiti, of ever hunting down my enemy. 'What should I do?'

'Get yourself locked up with the other mad bastards,' came a reply from a curtained bunk.

Well, others must have heard that man and agreed – it's what they did to me.

It seems like only moments before.

It seems like years and years have crawled past.

I have done all that they asked of me. Now they will let me go.

They cannot keep me from *him*.

Good luck to the poor sods left behind in this room. I touch the back wall. God bless those who live no more. I touch the window. I should have done more but I'm only a marine. I obey orders and I fight. I fight.

I smell burning powder, burning flesh, the stink of battle. I've smelt it since Old Man Hooke's death and Fleet's theft of his only treasure.

A man in the corner of the room says, 'You low down dog, James Norris.'

I shout, 'What did you say?'

He shakes his head, won't look at me.

'Coward so you are,' a man on the shit bucket hisses.

'Left Hooke to die,' says another man shuffling on all fours. 'Too scared to kill Fletcher.'

I know they say these things even though their lips don't move.

All I have to do is stay quiet, stay still.

Footsteps echo in the passage.

The key clicks in the lock.

The burning smell makes me cover my face with my hands. Opening my fingers a crack.

My head is in mutiny, the day splits in two: I see one way through my starboard eye, see another way through my port eye...

If I turn I will see Fleet with the key. He will trip into Parrot Boy flapping by the door. He will slap him about the head. Enjoying himself. He'll call Rodley to fetch me.

Rodley will see Fleet is busy, he won't want to come through the room on his own. He'll wave to me, and I'll go towards him.

I'll keep my mouth shut, walk past Fleet and Parrot Boy, the swirl of feathers and cusses that is their struggle. Rodley will lock the door behind us, push me down the passage.

I will greet Haslam with a nod, my mouth firmly shut. But my silence will make him glance up from his ledger. I'll see there are ropes I must climb. So, I'll wish him the best of it. I'll say I'm looking forward to setting to sea. I'll thank Haslam for his patience

If I turn I will see Fleet with the key. He will be smirking. He will come and stink of yeasty beer, all got from Old Man Hooke's guinea. He will kick anyone too slow to get out of his way. He'll call my name to take me over to Haslam to sign out. Only, when he touches me I know it will burn – the stink of burning flesh.

I will scream the sun out of the sky. The shit, and the blood, and the piss that is eating me up will explode. It'll mark the commencement of battle.

We will fight then. Him with his well-fed belly might get the better of me to start but the fog of drink and shagging will make him unsteady on his feet. I'll get him down in the straw, in the piss and the dirt. We'll both know that one of us isn't getting up again.

and care. Haslam will approve of such sentiment, sign my release. Rodley will show me to the gates. I'll step out into a cold but bright winter's day before the ink is even dry.

Rodley will come running. It will be a fight with punches, flailing, scratching, butting, and biting.

It will hurt.

Hell, I'll mean for it to hurt.

16

I keep hold. Teeth clamped. Skin, bone, in my mouth. Blood. A man howls. Running feet. A rope tightens about my neck.

This is how I die – in Bedlam, on my knees in the straw.

Is it now?

No?

Then is it now?

Can't breathe.

The keepers stand over me, tall as masts. No surgeon, no apothecary to save me. The crew – not one of them will mutiny. They sit or shake or pace – each man to his own hell.

Pull harder, boys. You'll never hold me.

The rope burns. They mean to split and spew me open.

Can't keep biting much longer. My tongue bulges. Mouth bursts. Fleet's finger rolls away. I spit out blood and gristle. Now he's lost something too. I'd laugh but there's no air in me.

No air in Bedlam.

No air in all London.

Keepers move as one. Punching. Kicking.

They think they have me? They think they have me!

A fist cracks against my head.

A scream slaps against the crumbling walls.

I taste blood, hot on my tongue.

A keeper punches my gut. Unbalanced. Falling. Smashing into straw and mud.

Might as well be at the bottom of the sea. I've been many places but never there.

A knee in my back. A boot on my neck.

A keeper shouts, 'Don't fight it,'

But I will. I will. But.

If I could puke out the words, I'd curse them all – the gin-soaked surgeon Crowther, the weak-chinned Haslam. What the fuck use is an apothecary with no potion to save me? The keepers, spare an oath for them: Fleet and Rodley. I'll take all their fingers. I'll gnaw them to the core, make them nothing but gore to be swilled from the decks.

I'll fight them all.

I leap up. Swing my arms free, knock the keepers back. Shirts filling with air like sails. Press my back to the wall. I scream, 'I'm coming for you.'

Brick and plaster crumbles.

The keepers face me, mouths open. Only Fleet, blood-soaked hand pressed under his arm, has the bollocks to come at me. He leans in.

'You're a dead man, James Norris,' he says, so quiet I have to strain to hear it.

I laugh. I died long ago, down in the mud of the Royal Garrison graveyard, broken easy as a corn dolly.

Rodley grabs the rope, slams me down again.

They kick my legs. Clout my head.

Blood in my eyes.

Everything runs red.

Something cold soaks into my breeches, tickling me. Listen.

Lapping of water against wood. I lie still. They don't know it yet, the fools, but I've summoned the sea to me – surging from the Channel, running up the Thames, through Moorfields, sweeping aside the gates of Bedlam. Water sails in under the door. The tide rises.

Gasping not for air but water. Slits opening along my body. Legs gone. Tail beating in the muck. Eyes slipping to the sides. Body writhing, scales scraping and snagging; struggling to reach the water flowing in under the door.

It washes over my head, between my gills...

Overboard. Waves part.

Sinking down. In and out of lives lived – past whales, schools of mackerel, tendrils of seaweed. But I can't float free. The line has me still.

I hang there. Can hold on, let the keepers haul me back, or –

17

Water all around. I'm at sea. I hear the lap, the slap, of it against the side of the ship. Fog hides everything, even my hands stretched out in front. I part nothing but wet clouds. My fingers disappear. Salt air nips my cheeks.

I only ever once sailed in fog so thick.

I'm there again. The Cape of St Vincent, 14th February, 1797, the log reads but it won't tell all.

The crew creep about deck. No man sings, or speaks too loud. Out there in the whiteness somewhere is the Spanish fleet. Maybe the splash of water echoes off their hulls, and they surround us. Maybe it's a whale song. The rail presses into my guts. I'm at the edge.

There's light out there. Dawn comes, eats up the fog.

The clouds now are from our breath.

I should be lying in the living green beauty of paradise. Or lying between Ruth's thighs. But here I am – because of Fletcher Christian. My red coat is streaked with dew, silvery like old bacon. Taste it in the dawn air, salted, stinging. The burn before battle. I stand on watch.

Appearing above the steam, like trees in a forest, rise masts. The Spanish fleet is formed around, battle lined, battle ready.

The ropes won't hold him. Fetch the chains.

Daylight sears through everything. Down below, on the gun deck, shafts of light tumble from the hatches. It starts as a whisper but grows until it's the only sound, 'The Spanish are twenty-seven sails of the line. We're outnumbered.'

I am beside the fifth gun, lower deck, when the signal comes. Engage the enemy.

Guns fire. Smoke more blinding than fog. A double dose of grog blazes in my gut. Mouth full of ashes, crunching between my teeth. I see no crew around me. Hear no crew. An arm knocks against my side. A foot treads on my hand. A head butts into my back. Trapped in battle fog. Nothing is solid but the hot metal of the gun. The boards beneath my feet tremble. A cannon ball hits water and wood...

Strap his legs.
Have hold of him, Rodley.
Don't let him fucking bite again.

...I'm pulled from behind, away from the gun. Who will take my place? Who will protect the ship? But I have my orders to ready for attack. Bayonets on muskets. Slip and clip of metal.

Signal to board is given.

Over lines. Over sides. White flutter of shredded sails, falling shards of bone. The enemy's deck is slick with blood. Smoke blinds all but the flash of blades and musket fire.

We're taking prizes, capturing the Spaniards' San Nicolas...

I'll make the bastard pay for taking my finger.

... I have my orders. What else can I do but stab, splice and shoot? Blood soaks into my coat. Red on Red.

I am blood.

Guts, bone, skin, swilling on the decks, I wade through it all. Each head, each arm, each neck I strike, it is Fletcher Christian's face I see. Hell is what he's driven into me. And I want to kill them all, any in my way. Every Fletcher Christian that stands on the San Nicholas' deck.

I shouldn't be here –

shouldn't be here,

I scream, 'For Paradise.'

No one hears me above the din of the dying.

A cannon ball explodes the sea into the sky. Staring into the blue all about. Don't know if I'm up or down. Water smashes onto the deck. The sea empties itself. Weeds and sand and fish.

Mackerel writhe, stripes flashing, breathing in the blood and guts, snaking their way amongst the dead. Captured on San Nicolas.

One flips over on my boot, gills flapping, gasping, eyes clouding, crying – Save me. Save me

try to pick up – hands won't hold – cold as blue ice – scales scratchy – body pulsing

save me

me

II

HERE BE MONSTERS

18

Bedlam, 1801 (or 1802)

We rage through the night. We rage in the morning. We rage in spring, in summer, past autumn, out into the frost of winter.

The ropes are replaced with chains. The chains replaced with a leather harness. It fits over the head and fastens at the back. The leather harness is replaced with a metal harness and more chains. The metal harness and chains are replaced with a stronger metal harness and heavier chains. A stake is planted behind the cot.

At last everything goes still.

We raged the year away.

Well, I think it's been a year, maybe two. Damned if I know how long has gone by.

I have a cell to myself.

I shift on the cot. The chains clink, sounding like the turning of a hundred keys in a hundred locks – suppose that's what it is. They sit heavy on my chest, pull back my arms, making a figurehead of me. I sniff but there's no smell of the sea. They don't want me going anywhere. And I could have got out... if that day last year (or the year before) had gone differently. It might well have happened like that: the pat on the shoulder; the good wishes not to return; the busy streets of Moorfields rushing up against me; the first taste of a meat pie and ale dense with the scent of oak. And Fletcher? I'd be no further from having that prize than I am this day.

But Fleet went and took that guinea from Hooke.

I shout out, 'It wasn't his to take.'

And that's how Fleet lost his finger to my teeth. How I ended up roped and battered on the floor. How I got signed over to the incurables, locked in this cell. No company but the Screamer next door.

The Screamer is quiet now though. I stand up, take the weight of the chains over my arms, get up against the wall between our cells. I don't remember coming over this side before. It is only a few steps but everything is different. The bricks feel wet. I press my cheek against them. The cold makes my teeth ache. My tongue crawls over the top row, finds a loose one aft. It tries to stick in the gum, but my tongue gets the better of it.

The grey tooth lands on the floor, a bloody trail of spit hangs from my lip. I lick it away. A musty taste like the last dregs of beer from a barrel. All those years at sea and I never dropped a tooth. Saltwater toughens most things. I press my head to the wall, lower my arm to scoop up the chain before it tips me.

I pick up the tooth, press it to the brick; low down near the floor. I scrape it against the wall, blow the dust away, leaving white letters behind. I mark each axis of the cell the same, fixing my compass points:

Fletcher did this

Fletcher did this *Fletcher did this*

Fletcher did this

I twist the tooth into the hem of my gown for safe keeping. What does it matter if I lose another piece of myself? There is only broth (nothing like a good lumpy lobscouse), the odd chunk of bread, not like I need teeth for any of that. My head and neck takes the weight of the chains. I line up my sight with the rows of brick. I must learn all there is about this place – must be a way out.

Drip, drip, on the other side of the wall. That's the Screamer. He drawls, long fat strings trailing from his lips. I've heard the keepers talk of it. I've not seen him myself, well I've seen bits of him – he likes to fling his shit into the passage. I suppose the keepers find it a threat to their territory; he takes as many beatings as me. I knew a sailor once always pissed on the wheels of the cannon before a battle. He said it brought the ship good luck. I hope the Screamer and his shit bring some luck to this dark berthing.

I run my finger down a crack in the wall. This place is rotten from the inside. Bricks crumble, limewash flakes, floorboards pop and rise in the night, only to sink again when I stomp them down in the morning. The window high above the cot has a view of the bowing roof from this side. The building turns a corner halfway across the back of this cell. Must be someone else in there. They've a window. It must let in rain too as there are only bars covering it. Not that it bothers me. The stake behind the cot gets softer by the day. A few more winter rainstorms and I'll get the better of it. Then there are only the bars to pass.

'Rain, you bastard.' The sky doesn't answer, just bloats with its own greyness.

I sit on the cot. The wooden sides stop me from stretching out. I lay the chains down, rub each arm, shivering at that bit of heat. I pull up my knees, hop to the other end of the cot. I want to see how far and fast I can move without rattling – never know when a bit of silence might be needed. The chain clinks, falls against the wooden stake. Always tomorrow.

I lie down, climb my feet up the wall. If there's another man in that cell behind the back bricks, he's a silent one. Maybe he's a late sleeper. Although this time of year it's hard to tell afternoon from night, and here in this cell it never quite gets light.

'Nobody, you up here too?'

I know he's somewhere. I feel it, a tightening in my gut, a catch in my throat when I go to say his name: *Fletcher Christian*. But I keep those words to myself.

I should have listened to Old Man Hooke. But do people get out? They must. And when I do, I'll have all I've missed, all I want. I should wish for breeches. I drag the gown over my legs, pin it with my knees. I bet Rodley got my uniform coat with its smart buttons. I know Fleet has my boots. May they rub his toes raw. I've not enough fingers to count all I want (but more than Fleet who's missing one – I still taste that in my dreams). So I have to use the links in these chains instead:

Ham bone soup
Hot peas
Grog
Canvas under my backside
Wash day
Heavy softness of a woman's breasts on my chest
A pipe
Fletcher's neck in my hands
Salt crackling on my skin
Ruth's hair

My thumbs digging out Fletcher's eyes
Taste of the sea on my lips
Ruth's cunt
Ruth
Ruth
Ruth, I hate you

All lists end this way. I begin to count the bricks instead, to get a measure of the place. Numbers never played tricks on a man, they are what they are.

One, two –

'I loved you, James,' Ruth says.

I know her voice. I know it's not there.

Leave me be.

Her laugh like the misfire of a tiny cannon – rumble, knocking back of her head.

Three.

Her way of biting her bottom lip when thinking something over.

Four.

Her scar across the top of her foot, brown and thick from the time her mother slammed the door on it.

Her neck arching when she came with me inside her (and it wasn't a trick – I felt that).

Her hands cupping her belly when she told me of our lost boy.

'James...'

'Shut up.' *Five –*

'You've been too long out there without me, James.'

'I'm done listening to voices in walls.' *Five, five, six –*

'I'm inside,' she says.

Her voice is so close, as if she stands behind me.

My heart beats like a sail hunting for the wind.

I look down, there's a crack between the floorboards. It crumbles at the edges. I get on my knees – a light shines there. The ground shakes, the crack gapes like a mouth. Wider. Wider. Nothing to hold onto.

How long before you return, James Norris?

One more voyage and you'll be Ruth Norris.

I fall.

Squeezing, sliding through. Mortar and sand stick to my face. It grazes my arms, scratches my body. I wriggle, crawling upwards now. Fists full of mud. Surfacing.

Back in Portsmouth.

It is late, too late. I'll get docked a day's wages for not making it back on time. Ruth won't make it to her lodging before the gate is locked. But we don't care.

A spring tide brings the Solent up to the lip of the seawall. Ruth reaches out her hand, trails it through the water as we walk along.

Moonlight trickles over the sea, making a giant mirror of itself. Its yellow glow coats our faces and hands.

'Do you see these stars when you're sailing?' she asks.

'And others.'

'Them others must be more beautiful.'

'No, these here are my favourite.' I stop, tilt my head, look up into the sky.

Ruth stands in front, leaning into me. Her face pointing up. 'What about the star on your chest? My name's not the first tattoo you've had.'

'The rose for my mother. Your name –'

'And the four-pointed star?'

I rub my chin, put my thumbs in my belt, clear my throat – the words won't come. Then I drop my face to her chest, the heat of her breasts scolding my cheeks. Ruth rubs my neck.

'It's a map,' I say.

'To where?'

My lips brush her throat; she shifts from foot to foot, pressing into me. Our boots touch. 'To you, Ruth.'

'You're making it up.' She tugs on my hair, pulling my head away.

Only I'm not making it up, not like I did for Fletcher – showing him a world he needed to see, just like William revealed to me the kingdom he created in the barn. I went off and hunted the oceans for what William gave me. Fletcher needed the same to get him through that night in the Atlantic – fallen overboard, fallen out of himself – not a lie but the truth as it needed to be. But now this is the truth of Paradise, of Ruth...

I open my shirt, put her hand over the four-pointed star tattoo. 'It's all for you – Ruth Norris,' I say.

'Don't make fun.' But she's not laughing. Her hands cup my face.

'Ruth Norris,' I shout it out into the harbour, no echo comes back. 'When I return we'll find the first church will take us.'

She lowers my face to hers. 'You are my starlight, James Norris.'

'You are my Paradise, Ruth.'

The spring tide turns as we find each other.

We laugh. We kiss. We navigate buttons, stays, ties. We match the lap of the waves.

19

My dreams crack open; I wake with water on my cheeks.

I am back in the cell.

I brush a hand across my face, chains graze my chin. They aren't tears, of course they're not. Rain beats against the outside walls, hurls itself through the barred window, high up behind me. It's night up there. Bedlam weeps for itself because no one else will.

I never lost a finger, an arm, or an eye at sea (and plenty do). Why the fuck should I lose myself here?

'Bitch. Whore. Cunt,' the Screamer fills the cells with his filth. Flinging words where his shit can't reach.

I won't answer him.

Where are you, James?

I won't answer her.

Come inside, James.

Memories sit inside me like seeds – no, like coconuts drifting across oceans, waiting for a sandy shore to be birthed on. They have a beautiful inside; filled with white water, salty like the taste at the top of Ruth's thighs. The green scent of her...

Rather the Screamer, rather his curses, than Ruth's lilting lies.

She's the rot in my oak, the worm in my biscuit, the rust on my blade. She's put a curse on me.

I crouch on the floor, scoop dirt, splash water, into the gap in the boards. I'll fill every hole, seal up every gap.

My fingers crack. My knees crunch. I spit and spit.

And if there is this hell, mustn't there also be the paradise I was robbed of? Why does Fletcher get it all to himself? I want my own: Mothers nursing by the fire. Children sleeping at their parent's feet. Men and women, families all together. Come daylight, all the food you need hanging from trees, rolling out of the earth. Surrounded by blue water, green hills. So warm there's no difference between air and skin, melting into each new day.

There is no other paradise but that. No other paradise. No.

20

I've the feeling it must be summer here in Bedlam. There's warmth to the floor, the bricks behind my back, and a salty, musky stink on the air. The breeze wafts cobwebs on my chains, lifting the silky strands, making it seem that my arms are unravelling thread by thread. My skin is already picked apart. Too dark to see the rawness but my wrists and ankles are wet, the water in me leaking out of the sores. A fleshy torn feast for crabs.

I could always take punishment but there's no reason for this, no reason for Bedlam. Such things would never happen on Captain Bligh's watch. He was a fair man, I never listened to the lies Fletcher's brother fed the Admiralty.

Punishment is the gateway, step through to the next day as a righteous man.

'What else was it you said to me, Captain Bligh, before you had me flogged?'

Captain Bligh stands at the cell door in his blue and white piped lieutenant's uniform, one boot resting on the bottom rung. 'Marine Norris, your red coat and bayonet should mark you out as a man of honour and duty, don't let others muddy your boots.'

The gilt buttons of his uniform sparkle in the light. He holds a lamp above his head as if signalling to land.

The Screamer flings wet slop, straight from his arse, splattering against the passage wall. Captain Bligh rubs a speck from his polished boot. I keep my feet tucked under the cot. Bligh would think less of a man who let his boots get took.

Captain Bligh paces by the bars. 'We are all grateful to you for dragging Mr Christian from the waves, but be careful that you don't drown in that young man's wake.'

Boots and waves. I didn't know what he was saying back then. The punishment, twelve lashes, I understood that. It hurt less than a wasp sting. It had to be given for abandoning watch, but, for saving a ship's boy, Captain Bligh gave me an extra ration of rum and an extra hour in the hammock. The ship's cat Davey came to keep me company and Fletcher brought me down some tobacco. He helped the surgeon tend my ripped skin, thanking me again for saving his life.

We would have done anything for each other back then. That was both a good day and a bad day.

The same with me, James – I'm both your good and bad.

I'm not listening to you, Ruth.

And Fletcher, even then, as he stuffed and lit me a pipe, did he know he'd betray me quick as a cat flicks its tail? Did he look at me lying there, with my flesh torn up, all because I left my post and followed him into the water, and think that one day he'd tear out my heart too?

Strap me to the topgallant, flog me with the cat o' nine tails, do something to take away this pain inside.

The lamp is back on the wall, the passage is empty.

I curl up on the cot. How many hours before the next watch?

Here in Bedlam, I am still a marine but only in my dreams. Let me find my way back into those times. It's even worth the pain of waking again.

I shut my eyes.

Water drips.

Men shout.

Lines creak.

Wind howls.

Onboard.

The bright red coat glistens. The weft bristles to attention at the shouted commands of officers and sergeants.

I am straighter, taller, redder, stronger, prouder than any cock.

That is my life; not the straw cot, the metal chains, the damp cell...

'Whore. Bitch. Cunt,' the Screamer starts up again.

I scream back, 'Shut up, you dirty bastard.'

They won't give me any peace tonight. The wind picks up all the cries of Bedlam. I cover my ears. A storm gives them cover for shouts and screams. Too many for the keepers to fight. They let us have such nights.

I shouldn't blame my crewmates for wanting a bit of shore leave. Those few sweet nights of drinking and singing and fucking. Land lovers never understand men of the sea, call us wild, drunken brutes, but it is only that we know life is short and there's so much of it to be lived.

I won't end my days in this hole. 'Shout out, boys. Let's dislodge the moon.'

Howling, screams. Bedlam rocks.

'Fletcher?' I hope that somewhere out there the storm carries the calls to him. I won't stop until he answers me. 'Fletcher!'

Too many other cries, he'll never hear me. But others can, and I mean to fetch them to me. Ruth tried to come to me, to trick me. Well let me do the same. There are deals to be done.

The keepers, the apothecary, the surgeon, want to keep me here while others traipse the lanes and roads of this sinking land, singing Bedlam ballads for their supper, but tonight I'll join them in a chorus:

I'll bark against the Dog Star,
I'll crow away the morning,
I'll chase the moon,
Till it be noon,
And I'll make her leave her horning.

21

I've been singing through the darkness; now like a cockerel I'm crying out to muster the dawn but that's not all. The singing summons others from the deep.

Fleet and Rodley stand by the cell. Fleet rattles the bars. 'Keep this up, they'll make a gag for you, Norris.'

I say, 'Tell Haslam I'll stop singing if he comes to me.'

Fleet mutters, 'Someone should do something before his singing drives me out of my own mind.' He rubs the stump of his missing finger against the bar; a clean sever at the first joint.

Rodley titters like a starling. A washed and whitened collar clings tight about his throat.

I place my feet together on the floor. Whispering and coughing starts up in the Screamer's cell.

Fleet shakes his head, steps away from the shit-stained wall, turns to the next door. 'He's gone and done it again, all over the place.'

Rodley shrugs. 'Leave him to his own filth. It's ungodly.'

Fleet gives him a shove towards the Screamer's cell. 'Using their words don't make you one of the great and good. Get rid.'

Rodley throws a bucket of water at the Screamer's mess. Who's the free man here? They walk away.

The Screamer chuckles behind the wall.

I can drown him out.

Standing in the middle of the cell. Feet wide apart, head up, back straight – I'm a marine and even Old Man Hooke saw it in me. Now let Haslam and his lot learn it too.

I sing every song, some not even written yet. Loud enough that a new madness sprouts in the cells, echoes in the passages. I'm leading them all: sea shanties, ballads, even the odd hymn chorus, humming my way through the rest of the verses that I can't recall. How far do the passages run? How many souls stacked one on top of the other? But they're no worry of mine. My head rings with it. My tongue swells, lips dry up. But the Screamer keeps the call going for me.

Fleet returns with Haslam, they stand at the cell door. Outside another dawn is bubbling over the rooftops. Fleet holds up the key but Haslam shakes his head.

Haslam keeps himself in the shadows. 'So, this is the troubadour.'

'With these chains.' I weigh a length of it between my hands. 'I'll go nowhere.'

I had no luck freeing myself, so Haslam must do it for me.

I say, 'If word could be got to Captain Bligh –'

'The marine.' Haslam taps the ledger under his arm. Perhaps I am on those pages but I want to see him write me more lines. He dips his finger inside, taps a page, flips back, then finds what he is looking for. 'Admittance states you were between commissions.'

'I'll give you names of captains.' I dig my fingers down between the metal and skin of my wrists. 'Word must be got to them. I've important news for the Admiralty.'

Haslam shuts the pages. 'The Seaman's Mission has your admission letter. No one has asked for you. You would do better to submit to Bethlem's orders.'

Fleet rubs his gut, thinking of stew and dumplings probably. Haslam fingers the cover of his ledger as though it's made of gold.

I let the chain fall out of my grip, take hold of the bars. Haslam stumbles back.

I say, 'Orders. Yes – give me orders and I'll follow them.'

Haslam shakes as if he expected better even from a fool. 'Those who are willing may help themselves.'

Fleet shivers himself awake, keeps hold of the lamp. 'Mr Haslam, you're not thinking of putting this one in your book?'

Haslam preens the hair about his collar. This ill-tempered, thick-skulled apothecary just might do me a service. 'Put me in that book of yours – they'll come running for me then.'

He tucks the ledger under his arm. 'First you must earn the privilege.'

Haslam watches me. I step forward. He steps back onto Fleet's boots. Not keen to lose a toe as well as a finger, Fleet pushes him off.

'Give me the order to bring peace to these cells,' I say.

Haslam glances to the dark stain on the bricks, pushes a handkerchief to his nose. 'You are a wild thing,' he says. 'But you might yet prove yourself.'

I nod. 'My reward should be a new neighbour.'

Fleet grins, chews on the skin of his missing finger – I've no time for his games.

'There's a man I met down below,' I say. 'Keeps a blanket about him, calls himself –'

Haslam waves away the rest. 'Bring peace and cleanliness.' He nods. 'And your reward shall be a new neighbour.'

22

'You and me, friend,' I say to the Screamer, my face pressed close to his side of the wall.

All know about the fear, the order, the rule, the life of a marine. But that will only get you shoulder to shoulder on the battle lines. There has to be more or there's no chance the man at your side will risk all for you or you for him. Trust and friendship – is what there has to be.

'We've got to have peace,' I say.

I'll leave his shit throwing for later. If I can keep him quiet the rest will come.

I sit on the floor, arm resting on the cot, gown caught about my knees. I've not worn one since I was a boy, sneaking out of bed to the windowsill, trying to catch some moonlight to read *The Boston News-Letter*. My father taught me to read so the Lord's Word would be mine, but the Bible never got opened on those bright silvery nights. William and me, we told each other stories of pirates, buried treasure, all spun from those advertisements for seed sales, and lists of sailings. Today there's only drab light from the city outside, but the passage is hushed and we'll not be disturbed.

'I've tales of high seas and low ways,' I say. 'The places I've seen –'

A splash and trickle on the other side. The Screamer pisses against the wall.

'Not one for tales of adventure then. That leaves my sails empty of wind.' I climb onto the cot just in case those bricks don't hold back his tide. 'Family?'

'Bitch. Whore –'

I bang the loose loop of chain against the brick, cut him off. 'Well, you leave me no choice... Romance it is. I'll tell you mine then you tell me yours...'

23

Inside, I have many memories of Ruth. Here are my favourite three:

The first didn't start out as my memory but Ruth had such a paint brush for a tongue that I came to know it as well as my own.

One Easter, Ruth was about eleven, a bright day that thought itself to be summer. Clouds skimmed but didn't gather in the sky, recent rain soaked the hills a dark green. Ruth and her brother stood on the beach at Colwyn Bay.

The shore was empty. The boats basked in the sun. David, her youngest brother, was only ten but strong as a lad twice his age. The rest of the village sat in the whitewashed chill of the chapel, being told what and who they were. Ruth and her brother would take a whipping for not being present but that day they answered to another call.

Her brother wanted to be a fisherman but their family had no boat. They picked mussels from the rocks, and fished from the beach usually, but not this day. Ruth was going to help her brother take a boat; it wasn't thieving because no one would know. The boat lay on its side, on the edge of the others huddled together like sheep. It wasn't neatly painted like some but on its prow it had a knot in the wood shaped like an eye. She picked that one, tapping it, whistling for her brother to help.

The hull slid easily through the shingle, seemed glad to be on its way. The bay opened up, throwing back its arms as they entered the water. The boat skimmed the surface more like it might fly than float. Their bare feet and legs throbbed with the cold splash of the sea. They clambered in and the boat settled on the small breaking waves.

The water was emerald like the hills behind it. Sea and land ran into each other until the whole world seemed afloat. They laughed, louder than any Sunday singing. They had an oar each. Rowing together. The bay, the village, the land – all retreated.

Once out in the mouth of the bay the choppiness of the waves bounced the boat along. She wasn't sick, not at all. The boat was theirs.

'Where?' Ruth asked.

'Far,' David said.

They pulled in the oars, black as jet from the deep water. They unfurled the sail, flapping like a mother's skirt but the thought was quickly blown out to sea by the wind. They thought only of themselves, perhaps for the first time ever, not about their cold feet, their empty bellies, the itchy nits in their hair. Clipping along, the breath racing out of them. They could go anywhere.

Ruth plunged her hand in the water. She forced it apart, bending it to her will: this way boat, that way water. She wasn't meant for that mean village life, waiting to be some neighbour's wife... look how deep and far there was to go. Her brother tacked the boat. Her reflection in the water rippled, broke apart. She fell back on the seat.

And she knew then she must always live near the sea, see it, breathe it, hear it or she wouldn't be able to bear all that life had for her.

That's how she ended up at Portsmouth docks. She always was wily, saw how things would go for her and hers.

Only that day in the boat, all bad things were banished to the shore. There was only wind and spray and the crunch of salt between her teeth – taste of freedom.

My other choice is from a dull, spittle-flecked day in Clock Street, Portsea. Only my second time of seeing Ruth. Those first four days on the boat together were more than a year before. They might have been all we shared, if I hadn't promised to bring back a coconut for an old salt I'd sailed with as a lad. He said he wanted one more taste of his seafaring times before he died on land. And if I hadn't returned from the voyage too late to grant him that wish, and hadn't been walking down Clock Street with the thought of selling the coconut to some soft sort as a giant seed for a giant fruit and get me some easy fortune, then maybe I wouldn't have found Ruth again. Funny how things go.

The rain was light, carrying the smell of tar off the boats. Summer bonnets and skirts rustled. I stood on the corner, drawing a crowd. I bounced the nut in my palms, let girls give it a squeeze as their beaus tried to break it with their hands. It grew stronger, the harder you pressed, but the crowd didn't know that.

I felt a tug at my sleeve, thought someone was dipping, and got ready to box their ears. But it was Ruth standing there.

She kept hold of my sleeve. 'You're back.'

Everyone else stared at the strange furry nut in my hand. Ruth saw only me. I opened my mouth but no words come out.

'Don't you remember me?' She wasn't angry, only curious.

'Ruth,' I said.

I didn't need the pause to hunt out her name or her face. I needed a moment to swallow down a joyous shout of recognition. I took a bow, presented her with the coconut. 'Man I got it from called it the tree of life,' I said.

She smiled but didn't try to break it open or play with it. She held it like it was newborn, cradled in her arm. If I'd have given her a pebble seems to me she'd have held it just the same. It must have been the sun coming out, blinking against the glassy brightness of the drying rain, that made it happen. But for a brief moment I saw her with a child in her arms and I knew it was mine – knew it like a deep pulse inside.

The crowd brought me back, jostling and shoving, spitting a few curses, as their fun was given away. Ruth took my arm, led me through the crowd. She left behind a third mate standing on the corner, though he was a surer bet than a baked brown marine juggling a nut for money.

I knew then what it was to be chosen – a glorious, burning, floating feeling... but dangerous too. I started to believe it was only right Ruth should choose me. Agh, yes that's where the worm lies – curled, sleeping, and hidden in its shell of furry happiness.

My third favourite memory of Ruth is all about one morning above the Three Tuns. Maybe it wasn't quite the morning but sometimes when we lay together time would sail away from us. Now this memory is all mine, and I never had to ask Ruth if she shared it too because she must – there's no other truth but that.

We lay on the bed, facing each other. Ruth's feet, warm at last, were pressing against my shins. Her toes wriggled and tickled my skin. Our breath began to settle, matching the sound of rain against the window.

It was one of those days when the light wouldn't appear. The room above the inn looked better for being blanketed in a dark blueness. No mouse droppings, no broken webs; clean and tranquil. The rope of Ruth's hair lay between us. I lowered my eyes, the room flickering behind the lashes. If I closed my eyes I knew she would too. But she didn't. Ruth's eyes were open, head turned from mine to stare at the ceiling.

She lay so still. Hair, arms, legs abandoned, as if she wasn't in her body, wasn't in the room anymore. A draught where she should have been.

I whispered into her hair, 'Where are you?'

'Inside.'

'Inside?' I raised myself up on one elbow. Her eyes held all the darkness of the room. She didn't see me.

'It is beautiful inside.' Her hand felt for mine. I laid my fingers where she could find them. 'Shall I tell you what I see, James?'

I could have got up, gone down for bread and ale. I certainly didn't pay money for her thoughts. But my coin had long since run out with Ruth.

I twisted the end of her hair around my wrist. 'Is it always the same?'

She shook her head. 'I'm at sea...'

She told me of a time when she was a child, of a day at Colwyn Bay, of racing against the very beat of life.

I wanted to laugh, pinch her lips, tell her to strap down her tits, cut off her hair and follow me to sea. Only it wasn't a time for laughing.

She sat up, held her knees, shook her hair until it fell over her face. It was as if she brought a little of that girl back with her. 'Know why I told you?' she asked.

I stared up at the damp patch on the joists, the rain starting to bubble through and drip on the blanket. 'Because I understand what freedom means, what we would be giving up.' That was what I wanted to think.

This is what I think.

Ruth held up her fingers, a drop of rain slithered down her palm. I licked it away. In telling me her memory she also gave me something else, something precious, maybe too fragile to hold – it got stamped on and crushed as easily as that little straw cross.

She ran her finger along the small tattoo on my arm, an English rose for my mother, along the points of the star on my chest. I rolled over, her fingers touched my back.

'I'm going to have your name inked there, Ruth. So, wherever I am, whatever I do, you'll always be with me.'

24

'I have a wife,' the Screamer says.

I pat the wall between us. 'Then she can petition for you. I had a friend said it could be done.'

'She's a quiet woman.'

'That must make for a peaceful home.' I lean back, twist my neck to see the window. The sun hangs low, snagging the rooftops.

'The only time she made a sound was when I tore out her throat. She screamed then.' He makes a choking noise but it's not that – a laugh breaks free. 'Now she screams all the time.'

I tried to be kind like Old Man Hooke but he was right again, never make friends in this place. The Screamer's laugh is low, angry. I thump the wall, which cheers him some; he turns to giggling.

'I'll tear out her throat too,' he gasps. 'Your pretty Ruth.'

The chain thuds to the floor. I stand up, press my hands to the wall.

He screams, 'Bitch. Whore –'

'I've a picture for you.' I rest the chain on my arm. 'So you'll know her.'

'Show me. Show me. Show me.'

I crouch down by the bars, his hand pokes out on the other side. I pass the loop of chain back on itself, form a noose.

'Have to reach more,' I tell him.

He stretches out his arm, long nails clicking against the bars.

I cast out the chain, catch him about the wrist, the rest he does himself. The Screamer yanks back his arm but I'm not letting go. A thump, a kicking against the floor. He's snared himself like a hare. No scream only a whimper. The more he twists, turns, the quicker it will happen. I hold on, chains burning into me.

Crack – his arm shatters.

'Picture me snapping every bone in your body –' I give one more heave; no struggle now '- beating your brains out, you so much as say her name again.'

All that time spent watching old salts tying knots over and over it turns out was a useful thing to do. He's panting, panting.

'Quiet,' I say.

I loosen the knot, enough for him to slither free. Slowly I slide the chain back into the cell. Spit out another tooth, knocked loose by all that struggle. I tie it into the hem of my gown.

Over the years I've repeated Ruth's memory of that Easter day to myself so many times that it's fixed fast like the ink under my skin, it's become mine in the telling. And I should have added up all the happy times long ago, kept them safe, as so much of the rest of life is only about battening down the hatches.

Ruth, you are both my good and my bad.

There is peace in the passage, for this night at least.

25

Love is like a wind, battering, edging forward, running aground on the rocks of madness. We even wish it away. But when the storm drops, all becalmed, pockets of stillness make it seem that the wind will never return, that all is dead. And we wish, wish it back – love.

26

For days there's been no light. The cell becomes sodden, easy to put my fingers through as mud. No matter how much I claw there is no outside to be reached.

It is around midday or midnight, too many clouds to tell which, but the wind changes, ruffling my cap. It is the mid-time of something.

I drape the chains over my arm, pace to the starboard wall, lean my ear against it.

The Screamer has gone. Rodley brings the new arrival, must be a gentleman as his clothes are clean, his shirt is embroidered about the buttons, his coat looks soft as a rabbit's ear. The keepers have yet to rough him and take what they want. The man's red hair blazes, his face hairless like a girl's, though his blue eyes are sunk deep in his head. Haslam follows him like a fly after shit. Here he comes down the passage.

'Mr Haslam, he's not the man,' I say.

He stops outside my cell. Rodley stands behind him frowning, plucking at his collar.

'And I said quieten a man not break him in two.'

'Should be clearer with your orders.' He'll never give me what I want, means to trick and betray me like they all do.

I have to get what I want, get Fletcher, get out. I have to.

'A mad man doesn't know how best to help himself.' Haslam opens his bag, takes out a small pot, shakes a pill into his hand. 'This will help with your madness. The new neighbour will help with your manners.'

He places a blue pill on the bar across the middle of the door, beckons me.

I pick it up. 'Then will you put me in that book of yours?'

I put it into my mouth. He nods, walks over to the next cell. Rodley opens the door for him, locks it again. Rodley paces outside. I spit the pill into my hand, stuff it down in the straw of the cot.

Haslam's voice is muffled but I hear what he says. 'Good afternoon, Mr Pomeroy. How are you today?'

The gentleman coughs to clear his throat. 'Very well. Yourself?'

Women meeting at the wine shop is what they sound like. Money – the man's voice rattles with it. I might get noted down quicker in Haslam's big book if only I had some coin, and the only way I'll find any in Bedlam is if it spreads from man to man like the runs or the pox.

Mr Pomeroy, how do you do? Mr Pomeroy let me write about every sneeze, every wank you do.

I spit, it hits the wall and sticks. Now I've got to look at it.

My mouth is dry, the water bucket is empty. And that's why I'll never be a rich man – I always waste whatever's mine.

Still, much good money's done him in there. I would have seen if they'd carried chairs, bed, drapes or more into that cell. That way lies a dead end. Everyone has to return past my bars.

His money only gets him courtesy and lies. But at least Haslam knows his name.

I lean back against the stake, close my eyes. If only I could close my ears.

Haslam says, 'Have you thought anymore upon our last conversation, Mr Pomeroy?'

Pomeroy says, 'Who's behind the press you mean?'

A press? Now here's something new. Down on the floor below I heard of missing bits of body, of memories like a leaking hull, of terrors crawling over the floor, of men who thought themselves made of glass or able to fly like a bird, of many things but not a press.

27

Turns out Pomeroy, Haslam (and me) have many a fine afternoon of it. Pomeroy chatters on about his press, a machine, that runs his life, that made him a spy of the French, who plan the downfall of King and Country. The press makes us all in its own twisted image, to do its bidding. Not printing words but deeds and people. He seems afraid of it but not enough to hold his tongue. The man loves to chatter, chatter about that press.

Haslam's back, carrying more steaming potion for purging. I'm surprised Pomeroy hasn't turned himself inside out with all the puking. At least that way he could slither, and slip his way out of this place, sloshed away like innards from the slaughterhouse into the street. If a man of money can't get out of Bedlam then there's no hope for the rest of us. Mustn't there be hope?

I run my fingers along the chains as I listen. To hear Pomeroy speak of the press it seems there can be only one in the world. Some may laugh at him, but I for one think there's something in it. What I've done, well there was nothing I could do to change it, just like this chain takes me to the door but no more – the press made me in its own image. What a helpful neighbour Pomeroy is turning out to be. He has more answers for me than Haslam the apothecary holds in all his potions.

'Mirrors and doubles, Mr Haslam,' Pomeroy says. 'That's how they have got away with it for so long.'

'*They*, Mr Pomeroy?'

Oh, Haslam's a wily one, he's spinning a great yarn for that book he's writing. That ledger he carries must be just like a Captain's log. I wish I was a hero in such a tale. But I'm not, so they leave me here to rot – my great punishment.

Pomeroy answers, 'They – the French who made me spy.'

I am a spy of sorts too, listening and plotting a way out. If Bligh or others should hear from me in here, hear all I have to tell of Fletcher – there'll be a pardon in it.

'I shall leave you a pencil, some paper,' says Haslam. 'Perhaps you could draw the press for me?'

There's the sound of something like a scraping, or a hissing, I'm not sure which. Pomeroy's voice drops low, 'What if *they* should find such a drawing? It's a plan for Paradise after all...'

Paradise – again – seems to be what many men hunt but can't find. But even some with a map, X marks the spot, would they recognise Paradise?

Fletcher's a fool for turning his back on Paradise.

Fletcher's a devil, got thrown out of Paradise.

What does that make me?

And now here he is and here am I, and really I've been here since that night at The Dolphin – for what is this cell but another room in hell.

The slap of pages and Haslam closes his ledger. 'Leave the drawing outside the cell. You can reach through the bars.'

Pomeroy says, 'Very clever, Mr Haslam. Then they shan't know it was me.'

Haslam carries a lamp. He stops outside my cell. He will speak to me. Haslam inspects a feather stuck to his coat. Perhaps he's carried it from his bed. He carelessly blows it away like any man who has no doubts about his own comfort would. Though he doesn't look a contented man: forehead forcing down his eyebrows, flaring out his nostrils. I stand up. Haslam lifts his head, hands over another blue pill. I've nearly a full regiment of them now.

He will speak to me.

Rodley, squinting and sniffing, appears at Haslam's side. 'Can I try the tooth key now?'

'I have to write up my findings.'

Rodley points at me. 'Don't seem right to leave him in pain.'

I shake my head. 'Nothing wrong with my teeth.'

'If I learn it proper, I could be more use to you. Do those small bits that leaves you time for writing.'

Haslam nods, opens his bag and hands something to Rodley. 'Be quick. All the tools must be put away before I leave.'

Rodley picks up his stick, thrusts me back from the bars. Haslam watches me. I must be better than I am. No savage will ever draw his attention. I've sailed with gentlemen. Rodley unlocks the cell.

'Sit on the cot,' he says. 'Hold up your hands.'

Haslam opens his ledger, writes something down. I do as Rodley says. He locks the chains to the stake. Shackled tight.

'Mr Haslam,' my voice breaks into a cough. I call out, 'Where's Nobody?'

He stays in the middle of the passage but turns an ear towards me. 'It isn't a place, man.'

I mustn't shout, but I lick my lips, try again. 'Nobody is a man. He'll probably not remember I'm looking for him. But if you should see him –'

'You say he visits you here?' Haslam takes a step towards the door, hand about the ledger he carries with him. 'Does he walk through walls or appear in dreams?'

'We were locked up together my first year here.'

A sigh slips from Haslam's lips. 'It would be better if you thought more on yourself and your own cure.'

'This Nobody – he isn't – I know who he is. Perhaps it would help his cure to know it too.'

Haslam opens his ledger again. 'There are several men here who don't know themselves.' He runs his finger along lines, flicks pages. 'None are unclaimed.' His hand drops away.

If I told him of Fletcher Christian he'd take that for himself, never mention to no one it was me gave him that key, and he'd use it to lock me up forever, to silence me. He tucks the ledger under his arm. Or maybe Haslam's in on it too, they mean to keep me here no matter what I do.

Haslam walks off without another word. I strain against the pull of the metal for a moment but I can't hold out. My neck trembles. My head snaps back.

Rodley has locked me up tight. Legs, arms, neck. Trapped. Wait, I can move my fingers. Can't reach Rodley. But I won't make a sound. He'll not get any pleasure from me. He puts his knee on my legs, elbow on my shoulder. What's that in his hand? A knife with a curled blade. I've had worse cuts from a bayonet, five times that size. He fits a stick into my mouth, fastens a leather strap over my head.

Rodley's face is close, too close to see. 'Struggle if you like. Makes no difference. I mean to get me some teeth.'

The fool could help himself to the small pile tied into my gown. But the hunt is what he wants.

'Fleet thinks he's the boss but he's nothing. He'll rot in this place.' The blade grazes my tongue; he shifts it against a bottom tooth. 'Not me. I'm set for better things. Fleet can stick his charity.' Bone. A crumbling, grinding sound. Rodley grunts, presses harder. 'Fleet's no better than shit on my boots. I'll get myself an apprenticeship with Haslam. Then who'll be laughing?'

He's laughing as he tugs out a tooth. Feels worse than any punch in the mouth. Rodley holds the tooth up to the lamp, blood on his hands. He slips it into his boot.

'I need more practice. That one's cracked.'

He puts his knee back on my legs.

This pain is worse than any lashing.

Rodley's arm compresses my chest. He digs in my mouth. Something moves on his filthy collar. A black speck jumps, lands on the end of the cot. It sits there. It swells before my eyes. Now bigger than a fist. Now bigger than a cat, than a boy. I'm caught between the wall and the cot. It comes for me.

I beat my feet in the straw.

The flea keeps coming.

Legs kicking, rubbing together, rivers of blood under its parchment like skin. Ridges on its back thicker than any armour. Hairs bristling. Strutting on fists bigger than my head. Why can't Rodley see it?

I scratch at the wall behind me.

'Don't fight it.' Ruth's voice comes through the brick.

I scrape at the mortar, try to hide myself in the past. But fear has a reckoning of me. I can't get in. The stubs of my fingers bleed, no nails left to break.

Don't fight it.

The foul creature will suck me from this sticking place.

The scratch and rustle is deafening. It will suck the blood from me until I'm dry and leathery as hardtack. I bang my head against the stake, shake the chains.

Don't fight it.

Flea into monster. Man into monster. I must be such a beast to be so chained. I turn away, try to bury my face against the crack in the wall.

Have pity on me, Ruth.

Where was your pity when me and the baby needed you?

I close my eyes, hiding like a small child – if I can't see you, you can't see me.

The flea has hold of me.

You have a lesson to learn, James.

I feel the scratch of skin and hair all over me. It stands on my chest. I taste the hot bilge hole filth of its breath. I glimpse the horror of it, hands still raised, through the thin web of skin between my fingers and thumb.

Its teeth burn brighter than the sun.

It rips me open.

Our blood joins.

28

The flea jumps.

I see it, see it from the inside. Me in the flea. I am the flea.

A leap. A bound.

Over Rodley. Between bars out to the land of giants.

Need warmth, taste of blood.

Not these men. Not the bitter sup of their sickness.

Keep jumping down the passage.

Fleas find a way.

Smell it, like a trail of steam from hot tea. Riding a breeze, down a wood-panelled way. Spinning in the air. Along passageways. Down stairways. Hunting. Always hunting.

Nothing is good enough.

Not the keeper with his stick. Not the women sleeping in their cells. Another jump. Land. Land hoay. Burrow deep into a cloak. Smell his skin, nestled into him. He doesn't know what he carries.

And out into Bedlam's yard – easy as that.

Off through the gates.

Hidden against the bright orange of evening.

Free.

On the street. Fast away from Bedlam. The screams of those locked up fading into the spin of cart wheels, the calls of fresh fish, milk milk. London towers. Brick, stone, mud. See her there with the ripped skirts, the loose hair. Him, in the doorway, swallowing smoke, eyes blacker than poppy seeds. Kids piled up, spilling over the windowsill. Streets full of hurry hurry and much madness.

Buy anything, sell what you can, throw the rest away.

Side step the slop of shit and piss.

Laughter high up at a window.

Cling close to the musty wool. Breathe the body's air – camphor, iron tang of blood, bitterness of liquorice root. A new world. Terrain of wool, cotton, skin. Burrow deep into the prickles of hair, thick as tree trunks. Wrapped tight against the light in a canopy of cloak.

The giant carries the scent of his trade, dripping from his skin. Away from his lair to where – another hell? If he should feel an itch, a tickle – it could all be over with a pinch between his finger and thumb. Nothing but a dot of blood.

The heat, the dark – comforting like a deeper sleep – some time before life began. But to live, to feed. Work to do.

The sun, the dirt from hooves and boots, nothing can breach the dark wrapping. Work to do. A door opens and shuts. Different air, a warmth, a sweetness. Struggling up through layers. Out into lightness. Witness to a wondrous scene. From this crow's nest, unseen – family hoay.

Baby in a crib, swaddled close. But one arm waves in sleep. Another child, all plump rolls of flesh, plays with dough by the hearth. Bread baking on the bricks. Milk cooling in a jug. Daisies blooming in a cup on the windowsill. A face reflected there.

The travelling giant is Haslam. He bends to pet the child's

head, sets the cradle to rocking as he passes. Even at this miracle he doesn't get out his ledger, he makes no notes. He sits, rubs his eyebrows. Work to do. A man whose disappointment with life pulls down the corners of his lips, holding back any smile.

A door opens. In comes wife.

Scent of crushed lavender, and fresh yeast. She speaks his name, loud as church bells to my ears. Haslam nods but doesn't look up. The frayed hem of his cuff holds his attention. She touches his shoulder. He taps her hand carelessly, doesn't see the needle pulled from her belt. Her help ignored.

Mother, child, and baby, gives them only a brush of attention – the rest he keeps to himself. His fingers move on the table, scratching invisible words. He doesn't hold Bethlem in his head, carries it on his skin. Most hunt for a way out. He looks for a secret key to lock it away for good.

She asks him what he thinks of ham and potatoes. She asks him if he thinks the baby is a little hot. He shakes his head once to answer both.

Work to do, work to do, the child chatters to him, building towers of crumbling dough.

Perched on Haslam's collar. Skin cool, the warmth of the hearth, the home, doesn't reach. Bitterweed stink to him. Climb higher. Climb out.

She reaches to lift the cloak from his shoulders. Shrugs himself clear of it.

Lifted from him. Air sweetens. Giant shrinks as the cloak is moved away. He watches her hang it from a peg on the door. Rubs his eyebrows harder. No maid, no grand entrance, thinking himself deserving of so much more. He neglects what he has. Fool.

A last leap from cooling cloak to warm skin. Nestling between blue cotton bodice and pink breast. Sliding down into the scented crevice of skin. Cradled close. Drinking deep at last. Tasting longing, ripe love that might sour like milk left in sunlight unless he offers up some shade.

Bite again – sharing wants and desires. Soft sleep here, dreams.

29

Once, I met a mystic man in the Bay of Honduras who wore pink shells around his neck and gold bangles stacked on his ankles. He told me I'd only ever learn the hard way. I laughed at him, kicked over his begging bowl, poured grog on his matted, savage head.

He was right, of course – I'm learning that the hard way.

Learning that cheap tricks cost dear.

Learning that doing bad things for good reason is no excuse.

Learning that what you have before you should be more precious than fresh water on a desert island rock.

If only I had learned all this before I lost Ruth. Lost? Before I drove her away.

Send me a sign, Ruth. Something to show I'm not shipwrecked.

What else must I learn of myself before Ruth will come again?

And when I am myself – I hope the sun shines on her but not too harsh, not to parch her lips or crack her skin. Hope she is fed, sleeps easy with no growling hunger. Hope her child brings her joy and comfort, that as a baby he clasped her finger with his fist, now cradles her hand on walks to the bakers for hot buns and loaves, maybe chapel on a Sunday.

And when I'm not myself – I hope she dies a little each day

on waking without *our* child beside her. Hope for a vile lingering decline, still at the docks, hollow with hunger, paid only by the desperate and those who like a whore who'll allow anything and not put up a fight. Hope she cries my name as others call out to Christ their Saviour.

I don't know which self is really me.

I don't know who I am.

I do not know who can tell me who I am.

30

Blood dries, cracks on my lips, making it hard to open my mouth. I lost another tooth in the night, knocked loose by Rodley's practising. I'm keeping it safe, tucked and tied into the bottom of the gown.

A scratching sounds in the passage. Pomeroy and his pencil drawings. I lie on the cot. The scratching gets louder.

The noise is coming from the cell door. I sit up, rub my eyes.

Davey. I know it is his name as soon as I see him. Front paws resting on the bottom bar. He clambers over, toppling, tumbling into the cell. He sees me but doesn't come any closer. He paces by the bars, tail held high. I scratch my fingers in the straw covering the cot. Davey turns his head, blinks at me.

'Get that coat in order, marine,' I say, and he sets to grooming himself.

His ginger-tipped ears flatten against his head. He spies a spider. Davey hunkers down, head to paws. He wriggles forward, belly on the floor. The spider dances on without noticing. Davey's more like the bundles of hair Ruth eased out of her comb than a kitten. But as all cats do this one thinks he's a lion.

I lift the chains, slowly sitting down on the floor. Davey tilts his ears, sniffs the air around me. He must like the stink of unwashed skin, full crap bucket and wet straw, for he rubs himself along the side of my foot. Twice he does it before he returns to the hunt.

I'd laugh if I could, if I remembered how, but I don't want any sound to startle this little creature, or fetch the keepers. They might take the kitten away; whether it is really there or not I don't care. I want it to stay.

'Davey,' I say, reaching out to rub a white spot behind his ear. 'I'll look after you.'

It's not true. No one gets to keep anything in Bedlam, not even their own madness – there's too much of others' lunacy to soak up. My fingers slide under his stubbly chin.

A high little voice echoes in the passage, 'Where are you?'

The little voice comes closer, still calling. *Let it be some other creature on the loose, don't let them take Davey.*

Footsteps patter along the passage, too light to be a keeper. 'Where are you, puss puss?'

'So,' I say, 'someone's hunting you, the hunter.'

Davey pounces on the spider, lifts a paw – already gone.

'You have him.' William stands by the bars, pale hair and pink face. His ears shine red as if they're freshly scrubbed.

I hold out a hand. 'What are you doing here, little brother?'

He puts an arm through but the kitten is out of reach, stalking the corner of the cell. William turns himself sideways and squeezes between the bars. He easily slips from one world to another.

He stands before me. I lean back. He puts one hand on his hip, with the other dangles a finger over the kitten. 'That's right, father has the rest of the litter.' He speaks as if we were already deep in talk. 'He says they make loyal friends.'

I nod. 'No getting a cat to stay where it doesn't want to be.'

Davey springs up, jumps for the finger, lands and rolls over, legs kicking in the air.

'He wants to be your friend, doesn't he?' William watches me, waiting for an answer.

I cough. It takes me a moment to find my voice. 'This one lost his way.'

William bends lower to tickle the kitten. 'He didn't like being in the bag.'

I drop to all fours. 'You're going to drown them?'

William looks at me, falls back on his heels. Crouching, we face each other. His mouth open. And I've been the one to feed him his first evil thought, the first to have ever entered his head. What a lucky escape my offspring had never to be born and dragged low by me.

He bites his lip. 'Father said they were going to live in the kitchen.'

I push the cap out of my eyes, wish I could take back that thought of black river water and sodden sacks, and mewling. 'It'll be nice and warm there.'

'They come from a long line of ratters,' he says.

I pick up Davey, he curls into my cupped hands; turning round and round, in a whirlpool of fur. If I could save just one...

I press my chin to Davey's head. 'All cats like to go to sea. Warlords at heart, each and every one.'

William leans an elbow on my shoulder. 'All of them?'

'You can hear them calling it out to each other at night. *I am from a long line of ratters, royal cats, the highest in the land...*' Davey's whiskers tickle my palms. 'I think he's sleeping.'

William shrugs. 'Next time will you tell me the rest of the story?'

'I'm sure you'll hear it soon, can't keep a cat quiet for long.' I'm still holding Davey in my hands, can't bring myself to let William take him.

I slide over to the cot, ease myself up, careful not to wake Davey, nestle him into the straw.

William gets up but doesn't leave. He stands, hands behind his back, talking and nodding at me. But it's not his voice I hear.

There's shouting in the passage, 'Harry? Harry!'

'Here,' the boy answers, crossing to the bars.

A trick.

I reach out for him. 'William?'

The boy smiles at me, shakes his head. 'I'll come again, next time you'll know me.'

I force my hands under my backside. 'I don't think so.'

The Screamer is screaming somewhere deep down in the bowels of Bedlam. He's reciting to me, low low words. I strain to hear. He's saying spiteful things about the boy, about his failings next to my brother William. *I won't answer you.* That gets him angry, he hisses vile things. *And I won't hurt the boy*. The Screamer tells me I must make this boy pay for all that's happened. *It's my fault, not his, punish me*. I bite down on my tongue, stop myself shouting back. *I won't do it. Won't*. But the kitten is on the cot, my fists are clenched. The Screamer wants me to make them all pay.

'Found him.' Fleet falls against the bars, fumbling with the ring of keys. 'You hurt, Harry?'

The boy shakes his head. He's spotted the spider too, catches it, lets it run across his fingers. With his hands held high, a flash of red shows through his open jacket. An arm reaches out, as if it's not mine. The boy stumbles back a step. I have him, rubbing the hem between my fingers. 'That's a fine red waistcoat.'

'My father got it for me. My mother sewed it.'

'Do you know what them buttons are?'

Fleet's hands tremble as he opens the lock. He wipes sweat from his eyes, the better to see me. He beckons for the boy, keeps one hand on the bars.

'Marine's uniform,' the boy answers, opening up his jacket. 'My father said I got to stand proud when wearing it.'

Fleet edges forwards, arm reaching out. 'He's just a boy, Norris.'

'No.' I jump up. 'He's a marine. Stand at attention!'

The boy stamps his feet together. Davey stirs, blinking and swishing his tail. Fleet tries not to move, wants me not to move either. He thinks I'm going to stamp on the boy, squashing him like he was nothing but a spider.

'Come out now, son.' Fleet speaks to his boy but keeps his gaze on me.

He winces as footsteps charge down the passage towards the cell. Rodley appears waving a stick. Fleet holds up his hand, quietens him.

The boy turns as he reaches his father. 'What's your name?'

I shake my head. 'Not important. But I think this little fellow is Davey.'

'Oh yes.' Harry smiles. Fleet grabs him by the arm, hauls him out of my reach.

Rodley slams the cell door shut. Davey darts behind me. The boy is back on the other side of the bars, back where he belongs.

Fleet is right to fear me. I turn over my hands. My skin, my arms, my legs – I wish barnacles would grow and cover me. It would keep them all away, keep them safe. I've already hurt too many.

Rodley hits the bars with his stick. 'Give back the kitten.'

Davey sits up, growls, needle sharp teeth on display.

'Davey should stay there,' Harry says. 'And the others will live in the kitchens, won't they?'

Fleet smiles. 'Let's get them settled.'

Rodley nudges Fleet and winks. Fleet slaps the back of Rodley's head. 'How did that bloody handprint get on the wall?' He points at streaks of red on the brick outside the cell.

'I've been helping Haslam. What do you care if I want to better myself?'

Fleet puts his arm about his boy. 'Just you mind the price is worth it, Rodley.'

'He don't pay me.' He rubs his collar, threads poking up.

'You fool,' Fleet calls over his shoulder.

I press my face to the bars, watch them leave. Fleet keeps an arm about his son, so close that their feet knock together. 'I should tan your hide, wandering off like that. Should box your ears, take a stick to you,' he says, smothering the boy's head with kisses, stroking his hair, rubbing his ears. Is that the monster I wanted to tear apart with my teeth, and settled for biting off a finger? I suppose it takes more than one line to raise a mainsail.

Rodley fumbles with his stick, trying to bang it against the bars of the cell while the other two can still hear it. He wants to say more, spit at me, curse me. Rodley looks like he needs a good feeding, lips thin, eyes sunken; even his collar looks too big about his neck. Maybe there's been no pay this week.

Rodley taps the stick against his broken down boot. 'I know you ain't been taking your cure.'

I don't bother to answer him. I go back to the cot, rummage in the straw to find a few crumbs of bread, spread them out on my palm. 'Here, Davey. Have a bite.'

Rodley laughs. 'Won't find Haslam's remedy there.'

I push my fingers into the straw; the blue pills are gone. Rodley bangs his stick on the bars.

He holds the pills in his hand. 'Wouldn't want to disappoint Haslam –'

'You were the one on watch, he'll be disappointed you didn't catch me.'

Rodley stuffs his hand into his breeches, blinks hard and squints. 'More than one way to skin a cat. And the surgeon enjoys holding a blade.'

He leaves me and Davey in peace. No doubt, he'll sell those dots of poison to some stranger out on the street.

'Pay him no mind, Davey.' I gather the crumbs on my hand, bend down. He sniffs my fingers, whiskers twitching as he edges closer. His tongue is dry and rough. 'Eat up, boy. We'll be best mates, just you see.'

31

Davey teaches me to hunt.

Each brick, each board, each crack, each hole.

No Ruth.

But sometimes I voyage to where she has been.

Find myself back in Portsmouth...

In the graveyard, shame turns me to stone. Let moss grow on me, let bird shit stain me, let grass drown me, summer draught crack me, sea wind fade me.

People passing on the windswept street think me struck mad with loss. Ruth isn't dead but, despite the warm breath coming off the Solent, my heart burns with grief wild as the thrashing of sails in a storm. Ruth, I must find you. And as if in answer, something flashes on the water, the flip of a fin, glint of an eye – gone again.

How many years have I been here? The straw is wet. Sniff deep. No longer smell myself. I smell nothing in this place. If I could reach my nose, I'd check it was still there.

These things are still there:

thoughts

dreams

days
nights
winters
summers
springs
and Davey.

32

Davey yawns, hopping onto the cot, arching and scratching. He's grown big, too big to fit into my palms. Fur bristling in the draught. Is it forever February? Frozen in the bricks if not in time.

Davey nudges me a farewell before slipping back out between the bars with a flick of his tail. I wish I could follow. He cares nothing for yesterday, seems content with his lot – he is a good teacher. Is that a lesson I had to learn? I don't know much but that Davey's been the best of company, chases away my rages.

Some days there is other company – Fleet and Rodley. They ladle soup, salted with spit, drop bread in the dirt, hurl a curse or two and pass on. Then there are other days, like today.... the back of my neck itches, my leg twitches, feels like worms churning in my gut.

More cure is coming.

Crowther, the surgeon, wheezes his way along the passage. I've seen slugs in the cell with more hurry. I thought it was just me that time flicked and jumped around for but I've come to realise it's the building. Crowther's world must have slowed to the thick ooze of port.

He's coming this way. Listen. The drag and shuffle of his fat feet, squashed into riding boots, sound like oars snagging against a current. The faint glow from his lamp reaches the bars. They never leave me a light and there are no stars tonight. Crowther's breathing sucks life from the passage, not that there's much up here.

I wish Davey was here. I want to call him to me. It's not fair to make him return, but if he is close he might show a whisker or shake his tail – even give a call in passing just so I know he's out there, that I'm not alone.

Crowther stands by the bars. His eyes flicker and blink. 'How long has there been quiet?'

Rodley slides out of the shadows, ready to buttress up the surgeon should he topple. Fleet stands behind them, answers,

'Six months of peace this time.' He taps the stump of his missing finger on the bars.

Rodley wears my shirt, I sewed the anchor on the breast myself. He's the one summoned the surgeon.

Fleet holds the keys up to Rodley.

Crowther burps, the rush of air straightens him up. 'Time to make him respectable. Open the cell.'

Rodley grips the keys. Crowther burps again. Fleet shrugs, gives a small nod; Rodley turns the lock.

My hand reaches out for fur, fills with straw instead. Come back, Davey. If he were here I could share a wink and a jolly with him. No man gets between us two.

Fleet makes a show of holding the bars only half open. Crowther's too unsteady on his fat feet to totter sideways. 'Open it, man.'

Rodley clenches his fists, fixes his gaze not on my face but my chest. The light ripples against their legs. Fleet still has my boots. He's taken care of them, polished and laced. But they are my boots. He slams the bars against the wall.

Wide open.

The bang shakes dust from the bricks, wakes Pomeroy. He's calling for Haslam; Crowther snorts when he hears that.

Feels like my beard is sprouting into my mouth, gritty between my teeth. Ruth always liked me clean shaven. If she sees me tidy, more like a man... perhaps...

They come at me, one by one. The fat surgeon, nine-fingered Fleet, the coward Rodley. They come at me like they came for Parrot Boy – stole his feathers, stole his voice. Better keep their hands off me.

I stay on the bed. Under the gown they can't see how my knees are braced, my feet planted.

I could run for it, but the chains stay me, and I'd not leave without Davey. And Ruth – *Ruth, I know you're still here.*

Crowther's hands shake. He passes the lamp to Fleet, fumbling so much it must burn Fleet's hand but he doesn't make a sound. He places it on the floor. I've seen worse things than these men in my cell.

The blade is out, trembling in Crowther's grip. He wipes it on his waistcoat that's streaked yellow with yolk stains. He has drunk his years away. But still the keepers think him the captain. He licks the red blisters around his mouth, winces.

Rodley taps the button on his jacket, holds his breath to puff out his chest. Fleet strolls like he's off down the pub.

Crowther's voice is loud enough to shake the bars. 'We cannot allow order and cleanliness to slip, men. And why is that?'

Rodley replies, eager as a pup, 'It separates us from the beasts.'

Fleet bites his thumb in disgust at such grovelling.

Crowther sharpens the blade on a small whetstone; it sounds like splintering bone.

Something moves closer. A heat. Crowther feels it too. He's sweating. Drips bubble along the side of his purple nose. A beast they call me – when he's the fat pig, and the keepers are sharp-featured as rats.

I'll be out of this place before any of them ever will – one way or another.

Rodley and Fleet sway on the spot, don't know whether to guard the door or the surgeon. I wonder what they are keepers of – madness, I suppose. They keep us all that way. Fleet and Rodley keep their backs to the wall. This beard scratches me, and the hair on my head grows so long it's starting to curl. Let them have it.

I say, 'Keep a true hand, surgeon.'

Rodley starts as if I've just barked. The surgeon doesn't hear me. I am a dog to him. He'd no more understand a terrier yapping in his ear – or so he pretends. Fleet puts a hand on my shoulder, not firm enough to hold me down but to feel any movement.

The blade is cool, touching my cheek. He draws it over my chin. Curls, wiry as wool, drift and collect in my lap. He scrapes again, further down my neck.

I am almost clean. At least this way I look more like a marine than some poor soul on the Luxborough Galley: cast adrift, driven to drink the blood and eat the flesh of his mates. Although it wouldn't come to straws – a fleshy pot like Crowther would get picked first every time.

Now what's he doing with that razor on my head?

'Don't cut to the bone,' I say.

'The more they resist,' his sloppy lips drip spit on me as he speaks, 'the more good it does them.'

I hold my head still. Bet Fletcher, wherever he is in here, doesn't get skinned like a rabbit. Only the best for Fletcher, thinking himself such a grand one – his tricks and his lies. He'd laugh to see me this way.

Something hot dribbles down my neck. Crowther leans too close. Is that a lick of his cracked lips? Blood drops into my mouth.

Who does Crowther think he is? I serve the King and I'm sure as saltwater no madder than him. 'Be careful, you fat bucket of shit.' I say it because no one hears me anymore and also because it's true.

But Crowther takes this moment to unblock his ears. 'These creatures are a canker on God-fearing souls –'

I jump up, knock Fleet off balance, throw the chain over my head and over the surgeon. He's not going to spout more. He's not fit to kiss my bare-chilled arse. Not him, not Fletcher – but I'll get what I want. I yank tighter. Out there is Fletcher, I'll get my hands about his neck yet. Skin between links puckering and red like a line of little mouths. See how he likes to be chained – it's all that keeps me from getting what I want.

Can't stop my thoughts now, can't stop seeing what I want before me – me stamping on Fletcher's head. Eyes popping. Teeth splintering. Trampling his broken body into the dirt and the filth. Beating the shit bucket down on his back. Smashing his cracked bones into dust with the heavy chains.

The surgeon claws at the biting metal.

I drag him forward, brace my back against the stake. 'Unlock me, or I'll squash this bloated fly.'

Fleet stays close. 'Blacksmith sealed those chains.'

'You.' I nod at Rodley. 'Fetch the blacksmith.'

Fleet shakes his head.

I shrug. 'Or don't and lose your positions.'

The surgeon shakes. I loosen the chains a little, wouldn't want him to drop before I'm done. I'll be the captain of this ship yet.

Rodley laughs like he thinks this is a jolly show, probably wishes he'd put a shilling down on it. 'Drop them chains.'

Fleet turns about. I see Rodley over his shoulder and I see why Rodley laughs. He holds Davey in the air. Davey's legs kick out. He churns and turns trying to sink his teeth into Rodley. The tides are against me. Rodley grabs his tail as well. Davey hisses and howls, writhes to free himself.

Rodley tries for a man's voice, it rattles inside the cell, 'Put down the chains or I'll wring its bloody neck.'

I snarl, 'Put Davey down or I'll wring this bloody neck.' I shake the chains. The surgeon gulps and shudders.

Davey's tongue hangs out, eyes crossed in fear.

I drop the chains.

The surgeon staggers to the cell door, stumbling past Rodley, bouncing off the passage walls.

Rodley grins. 'I'll finish the mangy puss off anyway.'

I fling out the chains. 'Let him go.' They fall short of Rodley, the weight dragging me off the cot, to my knees.

Fleet backs away from me, reaches the door. If they do for Davey... He's rigid now, legs sticking out like branches, teeth bared. Not Davey, not him.

Fleet whacks Rodley across the back of the head. 'My boy raised that cat.'

Rodley drops Davey who lands on his feet, runs for the cot. He growls and so do I.

‘A joke,’ Rodley whines as they lock the cell.

‘You want to see Mrs Fleet cry too, when her boy cries?’

‘No.’

Crowther staggers away with the lamp. They chase after the light.

Fleet pushes Rodley down the passage. ‘Sometimes, I think I should have left you in the workhouse.’

The gloom swells the cell, pushing back the walls, hoisting up the deckhead. I drag myself off the floor. ‘All right, mate. Out you come.’

Davey pounces onto the cot. I sink down beside him. He purrs, settling himself into the folds of my gown. Nearly came close to losing what I love again. The material cracks, blood drying it into wrinkles. I peel open my hands, blow air onto the bruised skin.

Davey settles on my lap. We sit together, listening to the roll and rumble of his happiness. He kneads me. I harden.

‘There’s no harm in it, Davey. Aren’t we both glad of the warmth?

He blinks slowly, lowers his head, curling up. But I’ve no sleep left in me.

Can’t help myself. My hand slips under the gown. I’ve not felt a stirring for – don’t know how long. Useless as a broken pump. But I feel now. A tightening in my gut, sinking lower. Legs heavy.

‘I’ll have you again, Ruth. If I can just hold on...’

33

The next day, Crowther comes for me again. The keepers carry hammers, chisels, lengths of chains, a metal pole.

I cry out, 'Run, Davey. Run.' He skitters out of the cell.

Fleet puts down his tools, takes out a key. 'No one's touching the cat.'

Rodley laughs and I think for a moment Fleet is lying but he's been fairer with me since Davey's arrival. I stand by the back wall.

Fleet keeps his hand on the cell door, turns to Crowther. 'He were quiet before. He'll be quiet again.'

Crowther wipes sweat from his lip with the hem of his coat. 'Haslam's letting all slip for the love of that book he writes. This is my duty.'

'What we building?' Rodley jangles a bag of nails in his hands.

Crowther takes a roll of paper from his riding boot. 'Haslam showed me a drawing one of the lunatics did – a press or some such. I envisioned a better use for it.'

Pomeroy coughs, talks to himself. 'Those drawings were for Mr Haslam only.'

Crowther glances over at his cell. 'The artist. Well, there's no money to be had for them. I saw from the rustic lines how some practical mechanism could be constructed. Thanks aren't necessary.' He taps the drawings on the bars.

Pomeroy coughs again, but no one pays him any attention. He only ever speaks to Haslam, never to me. Well, seems I'm important enough to have something constructed just for my use. Surely that would be worthy of entry into Haslam's book.

Crowther comes into the cell. Fleet and Rodley either side of him. He knocks the wall behind the cot, measures the length in paces. 'Most of the work will be done in the cell behind here. But the wall needs holes and that metal stake will need securing behind the cot.'

Rodley peers over at the paper, nodding as if he knows what those lines mean.

Fleet knocks the wooden stake behind the cot. 'Seems solid enough.'

I'm not liking the sound of this.

Crowther shakes his head. 'It must be metal for it to work. Now, chain him to the bars of the door. There is work to do.'

He takes a bottle from his cloak, has Rodley position a chair by the door in the passage. He settles himself down. Drinks and watches as the keepers set to work.

They have a new contraption for me. All chains, pulleys and cogs. The machine they made fills the cell behind this one. I don't like the way the metal creaks and groans. It weighs my freedom. Pins me to the stake or allows me to reach the floor – all measured out by the length of chain about my arms, legs, guts, and neck. I should bark like the dog they make of me, but they'd take it for madness.

The chains lead into the wall behind, wrapping around the

metal stake. My fingers claw at the hammered holes in the brick. Pomeroy might call that pulley and cog machine a press, but what it is is more punishment.

I was better off with the Screamer, at least his crap never reached me. Now I find myself in a big stinking pile of Pomeroy's shit, his drawing brought to life. On the other side of the wall, the keepers scratch about like rats.

Crowther rubs his fat chin, claps his hands. 'The King himself would find relief in such a harness. I will put it to the Board. See how Haslam likes my success.' He calls up to the high window, 'Secure the chains.'

Crowther stands in the middle of the cell, the bottle in his hand nearly empty. Behind him the door is wide open. He grins. 'If you reach it, you can go.'

I stumble forward. The chains catch me at the edge of the cot. Can't go further. I cry out. Heave the chains, scraping my skin. Anchored. The collar digs into my throat.

'Leave me loose. Won't do anything,' I hiss.

My suffering fills the sails of this machine. My pain gives it speed. My misery will bring Pomeroy's paradise to life just like it did for Fletcher. He set course for Paradise and I got sent to hell.

If I could move from the cot, if the chains allowed it, I could place my hands on the compass points of this cell. I strain forward but all I see, scratched into the wood of the floor, under the rusted metal bars of the door, Fletcher's name faded near to nothing, and all that remains:

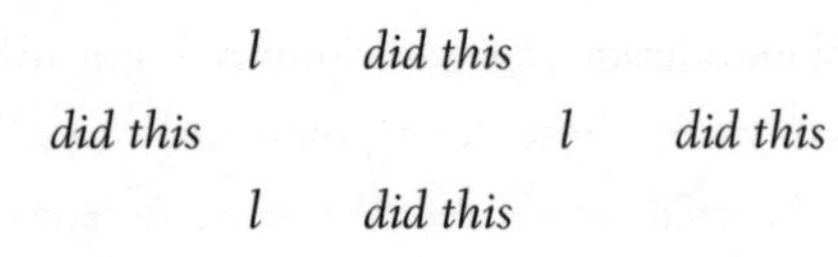

I fall back against the cold metal stake.

Footsteps. The cogs growl. That bastard Rodley chuckles behind the wall.

Hauled back against the stake, chained tight.

The metal screeches. Crowther walks about me, checking the shortness of the chains. Satisfied, he leans over, whispers, 'Madness is the freedom granted you. Go where you please, do what you want...' He raps his knuckles on my shorn skull. 'In there.'

Fleet shakes his head, locks the cell. He follows Crowther down the passage.

Rodley yanks on the chains from behind the wall. He tightens the pulley, though the chains will go no more. He squeezes the walls of the cell around me. He loosens and tightens the chains one after the other; arms and legs rising and falling, head flopping and jerking. He makes a dancing puppet of me.

My eyes are fit to burst. Rubbing metal, back and forth, back and forth. Fire in that friction. No water to cool the burn. Skin red. Bubbling, blistering. *Water. Water.* Won't give Rodley the satisfaction to hear my cries. I am threaded through with white hot metal, smoking like a blasted cannon. Skin bursting, melting, running over the edge of the cot, down into the grooves of the floor. Flayed. White bone shining beneath.

I am on fire.

Let me in, Ruth. I die out here. Ruth!

Stretched so tight, the star bursts out of my chest. It hangs above the cell door, dimmed but not dark. Paradise, the map Fletcher plotted from the descriptions I gave. I see it clearly for the first time, those four points. My north, south, east, and west:

Mother – stands at the edge of the pond, swollen ankles cooling in the green water, arms wrapped around the heavy load of child inside her.

William – fingers picking apart feathers and sticks, laying each carefully on the barn floor, building cities, flooding oceans, sculpting peaks, treasure chests full of precious gems laid out before him.

Fletcher – floating in the water, head tipped back to the blackness above, hands gripped tight to the body in front of him, feeling each wave as the bump of a shark, the swallow of a whale, trying to think only of Paradise.

Ruth – is everywhere, is everything.

The cot burns, the stake blazes, flames licking the brick, curling over the deckhead. Everything burns, the world white as its heat. Blinding.

Nowhere to look but inside myself.

And inside my lips will sail across Ruth's nipples, down again to her belly. My tongue smooth and strong like a prow through water.

I never should have left you, Ruth. I had everything, arse, tit.

Something flutters in a crack in the wall. Small as a dot, low down on the second row from the bottom. It pulls me closer like a turning current. Getting warmer now. The hole widens to the size of a pea, a walnut, a fist. A fleck of worn plaid pokes through. A petticoat. The split in the mortar now wide enough to fit a woman's boot. Feel, is that the tip of the cracked leather toe? The buttons undone, the boot worn silky and soft enough to roll at the ankle. A leg next.

Ruth's coming.

The rumpled hem of her gown shows. *Take me with you, Ruth.*

I rub the roughened material between my fingers. The petticoats quiver. A hand, bursting through the heap of skirts, brushes against me.

Fingers beckon. Out slides an arm, small and warm, protruding from the cell wall behind me. All I have to do is take Ruth's hand.

34

And I do take her hand. I grab hold of Ruth – warmth like wrapping my hands around a mess kettle on a cold Atlantic dawn.

Free. I tumble forward into her skirts. Shake my head.

We surface into a shaft of daylight, laughing.

Ruth brushes her skirts, hands coming to rest on her hips. 'Call this a room?'

'Fo'c'sle,' I say.

The other sailors and marines are burrowing into their hammocks, lasses swinging in their arms, rolling together. Still movement in the bones of the ship despite being anchored at Spithead, protected from all winds except a south-easterly. I bite my lip, think for a moment that the girl deserves better than this.

'Love, I don't need a castle,' Ruth says.

She's acting like the others, with a jutting hip and straight gaze. She's only young but makes me feel like the boy, like this is my first time, but that's not true for any here.

We have four days under the boards of the ship. A time for choosing a favourite, but mine was a plump girl who's gone off to marry an innkeeper and I wished her the best of it – we were good mates. But this little Welsh bit, this Ruth, looks like she's never been to sea.

I take her hand, tacking through the low slung hammocks until we reach mine. Ruth rests against the ropes; they creak and sway. The ship's cat, Davey, lies curled asleep; he pays us no mind.

Ruth stares at him.

'I can get him to leave,' I say.

She shakes her head. 'I like cats. Only seems to me he's the only still thing down here.' Her hand grips the canvas, knuckles white.

I press the back of my hand to her forehead. 'Do the boards jump?' She nods. 'And a sharpness like soured beer at the back of your throat?' She nods again.

Her face is turning white as boiled whale bone ready to be carved. My mess mate, Marwood, moves aside his girl's head. 'Get rid or she'll never earn a crust again.'

Ruth takes my hand. 'Did I do something wrong?'

No time to answer. I drag her towards the ladder. Ruth's breathing heavy now. I go first, hauling her up. Always best not to get behind a person at such times, never know what might fall on your head.

Up, up we go. A waft of salt air. Nearly there.

Sun scorches the deck, blinding me, but my feet know where they're heading. Ruth shakes, braces herself against the deck rail. I thump her back to make sure she misses the hull. She struggles for a moment but there's no fight to be had. She pukes. It splashes into the water below.

I hold the thick rope of Ruth's hair back from her face.

She blows again. Her back heaves, her hands tremble, but at last she seems to sway a little with the movement of the ship. There's a breeze dancing off the wave caps. She tilts her face to catch the play of it. I feel a deep pulsing in my gut. But it's not a sickness I've caught off her. Standing on the deck heavy-limbed with dread, lightheaded with joy. Ruth is my sickness, I know it.

Her eyes open, blinking against the blue brightness to find my face. 'You ever felt like this?'

I shake my head, this is the first time and that's the truth of it. But she's waiting for some other answer. 'Bad luck for a woman to get sick on ship. They'd not let you back again.'

'I never got like this out on the boats with my brother.'

'You'd have been leading a skiff. This huge beauty she leads you.'

Ruth nods, wipes the back of her hand across her mouth. I pass her the bottle from my belt. She takes a swig.

'Best to spit,' I say.

She aims over the side, forms an arc. And when she turns to look at me, some might shout at me to get away, shamed by letting themselves be seen that way. Some might just offer to shake me out before making for shore.

Ruth turns, face glowing in the sunlight, says, 'Spithead.' She laughs.

She laughs with such joy that it leaps into me with the violence of a lightning strike. I take her arms, swing her away from the edge towards the coiled up ropes. Her plait unravels at the neck. The ribbons of her dress flutter against my chest. I fall back onto the ropes, bringing her to my lap, keeping her skirts clear of the tar. Nothing should stain her.

We tilt our faces to the sky, deeper and brighter up there than any ocean.

We have four days together.

We make ourselves a nest as padded and warm as any rat beneath the boards. We fuck, of course we do, it's what we're here for.

Four days of joy with my Welsh Ruth.

We whisper so many things together. We listen to other grunts and groans, and we feel sure, as the horse must feel in the farmyard – we are better, faster, shinier, cleverer than the low beasts we find ourselves stabled with. What we find, when our tongues search skin, lips move over each other, can't have been found before. I've never had such wind in my sails, such treasure in my hands.

After those four days I sail again. Four days of happiness that leave us ill-prepared for the unhappiness which must follow.

The first time Ruth leaves we keep our gaze on each other as she steps into the launch. Her dark eyes wet as the sea.

She calls out to me, 'Huryl fawr. The cat will keep you company.'

'Huryl fawr,' I return, in the Welsh she taught me.

The pull of the tide is too strong, waves jump, and Ruth is drawn away from me.

Before the day is done, the ship sets sail out of the harbour. Taking the Brouwer Route. Heading for West Africa, around the Cape of Good Hope, running the easting all the way to Indonesia.

The old salts stand on the main deck, chucking coins from shore leave overboard, throwing away bad luck. I watch them sparkle and splash in the ship's wake.

I keep my coins hidden in the seams of my hammock. Saving them for my return to Ruth. I stand and watch those old fools, rotted through with their superstitions.

I laugh. 'I should jump over and take them coins for myself.'

The old salt beside me shakes his head, mouth open as if a dark shout will spill out. I pat him on the back, and head below deck.

Back then, I didn't understand the terror of bad luck.

35

Ruth comes when she can. When she does it's a slipping sideways into another place. There is more of this world to see than those who call themselves not mad tell us there can be – such misery only chains them to their own small lives.

This night, Ruth brings moonlight with her. Standing beside the stake, smoothing her skirts and hair. She looks only at me, into me. Her dark hair flames in the white light. So bright I lift my hand to shield my eyes. She pushes it down again, sits next to me on the cot. Her skin is hot, fingers holding my wrist. She smiles, but her eyes narrow. I want to ask her what's wrong, but she places a finger across my mouth. She glances over her shoulder, bites her lip. She takes straw from the cot, presses it into the crack as if there's something on the other side of the wall that mustn't come through.

Ruth takes my hand. The chains can't hold me.

Ruth raises me from the cot.

Ruth leads the way.

Ruth wants me to show her where the new rooms are.

Bedlam expands around us. Rooms sprout like mushrooms.

Doorway after doorway unfurling, leading from the passage outside this cell which buds more windows each night.

Each door I open I ask myself, what will I find in here?

We stand at the first door. My hand about her waist, her hand holding the back of my gown.

In this first room we find a bed, a washstand, a chair with a broken back. The floor is swept clean, the blankets smoothed flat. This is ours, Ruth says. This comb. This blanket. This candlestick. She names all the things, and things that only appear when she calls out to them. A baby cries, softly, distantly... not in this room but another place. Ruth doesn't name it and the crying stops.

Inside this room another grows. We enter it together.

There is nothing in the room but sea mist so thick that we fall into it and it holds us up. Floating on clouds, we lie side by side. Hands touching, feet touching – star-shaped.

Above us the North Star glows so bright it warms our faces, makes the sea mist sparkle. I turn my head. Ruth is close enough to taste. My mouth finds hers. The honeyed sweetness of a bursting fig. Press my nose to her cheek, and her smell is the sharp green of rosemary like that in her hanging pocket. My hand on her neck, the warmth of Paradise on my skin. It is beautiful.

I want to stay in this first room but Ruth squeezes my fingers, leads me on.

A second room is full of golden ribbons, thick beds of it like seaweed. Flapping, waving, streaming through the room. Tendrils that wrap and swirl about us, trying to haul us deeper in. Ruth pulls me back, slams the door shut.

Another door opens but Ruth bars the way with her outstretched arm. She shakes her head. 'Your mother waits but knows you have things to do,' Ruth says. I peek into the room. My mother sits in a rocking chair, a bundle wrapped up in her arms. I want to see who she holds so close, but all I see: a golden eye, flash of scales, flip of fin. Ruth closes the door, tells me, 'They're sleeping.'

She's rushing ahead, flinging open doors, slamming others shut. I can't keep up. She's laughing, having fun, until she's not, until the laughing is angry and sharp like the nails sticking out of the floor. I try to step around them but there are too many. They dig into my soles. Tearing. Slowing me down. Bloodied footprints left behind.

I open my mouth, call Ruth back. No words come out, only straw. Cold and wet, spilling over my tongue. The nails in the floor thrust up, topple over. Mud bubbles through. Rising up around me. Sucking me down.

I sink to my chest, to my neck. Over my head.

I'm through. Standing in another place. Light rain falls, light fails.

The Royal Garrison Graveyard, Portsmouth.

There's an open grave in front of me. The mud comes up from there. The edge of the ground crumbles, pricked white with frost. There's no need to take me. The grave is full. Paupers tied in sacking. Bones. Hair. A corn dolly sits on top, broken and torn.

A hand settles on my shoulder, a curl of hair brushes my cheek. My feet stuck deep in mud. No going anywhere. Ruth whispers in my ear, 'Look where the truth has got you, James Norris – a house full of lies.'

She sits beside me as I try to thread those strips of corn together again. She kisses the tears on my cheeks. Wipes the blood from my fingers.

36

And when Ruth can't come, when Davey hunts somewhere on his own, I am left here in chains.

Don't know how long I've been here – in this cell, in Bedlam.

Haslam appears at my bars, talking, not to me of course, but to two fine ladies (neither are his wife). I don't get up, not that the chains allow it. They have me pinned to the stake. Haslam presents his arms as he speaks, waves his hands, looking straight ahead. The ladies wear neat stitched dresses, hats and gloves. He thinks he leads them, but their money puts a leash about his neck.

Haslam's cloak is new, no mud splatter on the hem. I wonder if his wife mops it clean each night, or if he has a maid now. Haslam doesn't carry a ledger anymore, he carries a fashionably turned walking stick with a carved handle. He taps it on the floor.

Haslam chatters on, on, on, and on. Doesn't anyone else want to spit in his eye, punch him in the chops, push him down steps, to shut him up? I try to press my ear to my shoulder, the chains hold me still.

One of the ladies says, 'You keep them well fed, Mr Haslam?'

They don't look the type to have ever gone without, cheeks like apples, eyes bright as blackberries.

Haslam smiles. 'Not too much. Gluttony heats the blood.'

That smile doesn't sit well with him, looks like fleas are stuck down his breeches. He shifts from foot to foot.

The women nod together. 'They must desire to be healed, your book says.'

Haslam says, 'We do not want them to get comfortable, for the outside world not to appeal to them, ladies.'

Ladies indeed, his wife is ten knots more the woman, with her plaited hair and flour-dusted hands, than these two brittle-coated almonds who smile, give open mouthed but silent laughs.

Sugared almonds, jam pies, jumbles, buns. I bet those women are soaked in sugar, boiled alive with it. I lick my lips. I could eat my way through the walls of Bedlam. The chains behind the wall groan and judder.

'Profligates,' one woman whispers to the other.

'More a weakness of will, my studies have led me to believe.' Haslam watches me. He's wondering how far the chain will let me move. He's wondering if I can reach the bars before he draws his guests away. He's hoping the keepers have me wrapped up tight.

One says, 'My brother has your book as well, you know.'

The other only listens to her own voice. 'Mr Haslam, is this man in your book?'

He shakes his head. 'There's nothing of interest in that cell.'

I never made it into the book, that much is sure. No one knows I'm here in Bedlam. No one is searching for me. They've chained me to this post but they can't hold me, not when there's so many places to go inside. I don't need to be found.

Haslam can't hold his smile any longer and puts out his arm to guide the women on. 'Now let me show you my subject for closer study in the next book.'

How Haslam thinks himself someone at last. I bet he strokes the cover of that book of his at night when he should be stroking his wife.

His voice from the passage, 'Mr Pomeroy, are you available for visitors today?'

'Oh, yes,' Pomeroy says.

'The ladies have brought some more sugared plums for you,' Haslam says.

I roll over, bury my head in the straw. At least I'm not a performing monkey to have my bars rattled, tit-bits thrown my way. Poor Pomeroy doesn't know it but he'll never be let out, not while Haslam displays him – talking, walking – an illustration from his book that's come to life.

Davey hears the thoughts in my head, his face appearing at the bars, come to offer his company. Grey flecks his fading ginger fur. Ice steals into his left eye, its milky stare fixes me.

He walks on his toes, his legs are stiff as masts. He puts his front paws on my arm, winks at me to help him up, which I do. His shifts in the damp straw. I rub the side of his neck. 'Better not eat too many rats. I'll not be able to see you again if you can't fit through the bars.'

Davey always comes to keep me company, and Ruth shows me how I'm not alone. And what I haven't yet learned to understand in my waking life, well she takes me by the hand in my dreams.

Ruth and Davey – they are more joy than I deserve.

Fletcher, what do you have? I know you're still here. Still alone.

37

Last night I woke on the Bounty and the deckhead pressed heavy with dread and below the boards cracked with hate and my back was torn from a wiping and my teeth ached from gnashing at fate that made my skin crawl with sweat and faded the star on my chest and it will fade and fade the farther Bligh sails from Paradise but I must have some of it and all of it and those that mean to keep me from it will suffer because I deserve this above all others but I'll share it if only they could see the Paradise in this life and how close we sail to its shores which I'd swim for save the sharks that circle so close and who would save me not that traitor James Norris?

38

Haslam and Crowther stand in the passage outside my cell; it is closer than I imagine they are happy to be to each other. They stalk and bump like hungry sharks.

Haslam shakes his head at something said.

Crowther sticks a finger in Haslam's chest. 'I've told the Board this book distracts you from your true work here.'

'My book will bring the Board what they need. More gentlemen – like Pomeroy.'

'I know you pocket extra from his father – wait until I tell the Board that.'

Haslam shakes his head. 'I have to get back to my new book.'

Crowther flicks his fingers against Haslam's shoulder but Haslam seems not to feel that slight blow. 'They'll never have you as one of them. Don't you know it yet? We're all tainted by the madness stain.' He takes a swig from a bottle, holds it out.

Haslam turns to Pomeroy's door. Crowther calls his name, grabs at the hem of his cloak. He'll cry, I swear it. His head falls to his chest, he staggers to the wall, Haslam's cloak stretched between them. He leans against that pull like a child straining away from its mother. Crowther stumbles backwards, holds tight to his bottle and staggers away. Haslam is left alone in the passage but he doesn't leave. He comes closer to the bars, stares at something.

I turn around. Nothing here but me, and Davey sleeping.

Haslam calls for a keeper.

Fleet arrives at his side. Haslam's speaking but I won't listen. I turn my back, hold the stake. He's never listened to me before, even the blue pills no longer arrive. Does he see me now?

'Open up,' he calls over his shoulder.

Fleet nods, turns the lock.

This time Haslam comes for me.

'I'll have that for the surgeon.' Haslam points his stick. 'Something to rouse him from his torpor.'

Fleet shrugs. He holds the door half-open. 'What you after?'

'The surgeon hasn't got one of those in his collection.'

I lift my fingers, move my toes – not dead. The surgeon wants me anyway. Cut me up. No body waiting for me on Resurrection Day. I'll never be born again.

Fleet rubs the stub of his missing finger against his chin, tilts his head.

Haslam tuts. 'The cat.'

My hand flinches to Davey. The white-flecked fur is brittle between my fingers. His back feels like pebbles.

'Davey?'

No shake of his tail, no arch of his body, no twitch of his whiskers. Wake up. Davey, I know you've got more than this to give. Show them the strength you've still got. Only a kitten moments ago, has it been so long? Fleet opens the door. Haslam strides into the cell, swinging his stick, coming for Davey.

I shout out, 'Surgeon can't have him.'

Haslam stops short, caught adrift. He's not ready for me. I strain against the chains, kick away the walking stick. He falls to all fours. I kick at his arse. If anyone ever needed a beating, it's him.

He whimpers.

'No one's touching Davey. Hear me?'

Fleet stands at the bars, leaning against the bricks. He stares at Haslam curled on the floor. He spits, wipes his mouth. He walks around Haslam, stands in the middle of the cell. 'I'll bury him deep.'

'Swear on it?'

Fleet spits in his palm, offers me his hand.

We shake.

He rolls the stick out of the cell. But he doesn't bend to help Haslam, he waits for me to see to Davey. And maybe it is madness to trust him but that's what Bedlam does to a man, turns us all upside down, Fleet too it seems – the years in this place have softened his edges – it breaks us all in different ways. See, Haslam there on the floor. He pants, crawls for the door. He thought himself a great man, wasn't that a fantasy big as any?

But I've no more time to waste on Haslam.

Davey needs my help.

Fur ruffling in the draught; could mistake him for sleeping but the legs lie stiff, the eyes, always open, always moving, are closed. I reach out. Whiskers tickle the back of my hand. I pick him up.

Holding him, I feel a kick in my gut as I stroke his fur against my cheek. I'll feel no more. So, this is the end. It had to come, as ends always do, but it still feels like a filthy trick. My fingers slide along the ridges of his spine, a thinness to him. I turn over my hands, a thinness to me – my bones stand out like knots and ropes. Slip a finger between my ribs. *Dead reckoning puts that final harbour not far off for me either, old mate.*

Swollen knuckles, white hairs standing out against the dark down on my arms, the wrinkles in my skin. My body breaks piece by piece: hair on my knuckles grows white; my legs are so thin they look like they must be far far away, not right beside me; skin peels (I no longer bleed) in rings around my wrists and ankles where the chains chaff; it must be the same about my neck and guts but I can't get a look at all of myself. Most of my teeth are tied into the hem of the gown I wear. I count five left in my head.

Time knows nothing of bars and chains, it holds us all prisoner.

I pat straw and dirt from off Davey's fur, pick him up. A heavy anchor to hold. I'll have to let go soon. Not yet. Soon.

Fleet makes an altar of his outstretched arms. I lay Davey down.

Fleet cradles the bundle, steps over Haslam's hiccupping body. He waits for Haslam to stagger out of the cell. Kicks the bars shut behind them.

Fleet keeps Davey close; his other hand grips the back of Haslam's collar holding him up as they walk away. Only right Davey should be taken out of Bedlam, maybe if I'd have let him go sooner he'd have had a better, longer life.

I shake my head. There was never any making Davey do anything. Cats do as cats do.

I curl on my side, ram my face deep in the straw until the hard planks of the cot knock against my forehead.

'Farewell, mate.' My words muffled by the wood.

Silence.

Silence does me no good.

When Fleet is gone, Haslam returns with Rodley.

Haslam says, 'This cell is for your attention alone. I want improvement.'

Rodley nods. 'Anything you ask, Mr Haslam.'

The chains creak, the pulley trembles. Hands dragged away, neck drawn back against the stake. Nothing to see but the deckhead, nothing to feel but metal.

'Leave me loose, whoever you are,' I cry. 'You'll get your reward. I've things to give –'

'Shut up, mad fucker,' Rodley hisses from behind the wall. 'You've not a bean.'

You never know who listens and who doesn't in Bedlam. Rodley laughs, yanks and yanks on the cogs. Hauls me back against the stake.

He fastens the chains. They mean to take it all from me – only what I deserve.

I whisper, 'Come boys – who's for the ever after?'

39

Winter comes hard and sharp. Ice clings to the walls, turns the chains to spikes.

I've seen things that no one else knows are here. Desperate, ugly creatures. Some of them bear my face. But the face I long to see, Ruth's, it fades slowly – her dark hair, the small chin that I could balance on my thumb, the dark eyes with golden flecks, flecks of red in her hair. She is all flecks and if I stare too closely the threads unravel, blown apart by the draught.

Oh, we had such fun – me and Ruth – onboard that first time, then again many months later after the chance meeting over a coconut in the street, in the bed at the inn, many times too. Ruth wasn't mine but we were each other's. I thought that was the way it would always be. What a blind bastard – that's me.

I neglected Davey just the same. If it's worth stating once it's worth repeating – blind bastard.

My eyes roll out of my head, across the floor.

My left hand runs like a crab out of the cell.

My head springs up onto the window, sitting by the bars: lips, eyebrows, nostrils, crackling with frost.

My right leg kicks, and kicks, and kicks at the wall.

My gut rolls onto the floor; it says, 'There is no getting back to Ruth.'

My knee bounces on the cot, collecting dirt and straw, searching for a leg to join; it says, 'Davey's not returning.'

My elbow whispers, 'You're all alone.'

'Now and forever more,' chuckles my cock as it curls around a bar of the door.

*

I wake into day or night, don't know which. My breath freezes between my gums. I'd eat my tongue if I could chew. No teeth, all tied into the hem of my gown.

Is there something softer, something with more give?

My skin flakes off me – no taste, no swallow – blows away on the air.

Only my tattoos hold firm. The black ink frozen into spears. Arrow tips piercing deep into my crackling blood.

Beneath that I'm hollow.

Hunger makes me cold.

Cold makes me hunger.

Nothing fills my trawling hand but straw which crumbles in my fist. Davey is gone.

Come home, Davey.

Cold or mad – it's all the same now.

*

Won't survive another winter here.

*

The chains are so cold they burn with silver fire – all pain and no heat. They are the only light.

The cell is full of all the children Ruth and I never had.

They are tiny but perfect. No hair, sealed eyes – like fresh-born kittens. They clamber over me. Too many to count. So soft.

If I listen carefully they tell me their names. William. Ruth. David. James. Elwyn. Anna. I try to keep them all in my head but they tumble out, too slippery to hold.

Half-formed little fingers stroke my chest, fiddle with the rotting gown, pinch my face, squeeze my eyes shut, tug at the grey hairs on my chin.

Scratching, trying to bite, but feeling like the suckle of fish.

They blame me for the life that never came. They claw at my cheeks, faces screwed into a red mask of anger, the screams pitched too high to hear. They beat my chest, searching for my heart. They kick my head, pleading for me to sing out their names.

Fingers, nails, feet, all so small they give me no pain. And that is more pain that I can bear.

*

Not survive another night here.

*

Not American.

Not English.

Not son.

Not brother.

Not husband.

Not father.

Not marine.

Not living.

All ghosts here – half-life creatures.

40

'Wake up, Norris.' Fleet puts the bucket down, nearly drops the bread in it as he looks into the cell. 'Fucking Rodley.'

He leaves the water and bread outside. He's gone, back down the passage. Maybe this is some new cruelty to tempt me with food and water – some test of Haslam's.

The chains drop loose about me. I slip forward on the cot. I try to steady myself but my arm shakes. It takes a moment but I ease myself to the floor. Boards and straw, never felt so good. Spread out my legs like kicking against water.

Fleet is back, picks up the bucket, opens the cell. He's nothing to fear from me, the chains only reach to this spot halfway between the cot and the door. The dampness of the bricks is good as any rain, it trickles down my back.

'Shouldn't have happened,' Fleet says. 'Rodley were told to let the chains out.'

I rub life into my arms. I try my feet on the floor but my legs tremble, let them slide away again. Fleet ladles water into my pail, he throws a hunk of bread into my hands. It is still warm from the oven. Now I am awake, now I am warm, I must keep my sense, must find a way to free myself of this place, or next time I might not surface.

He says, 'Rodley's been going round, telling all you've money hid away.'

I swallow, wipe crumbs from my lips. 'Not hid in here.'

'You'd do well not to put thoughts in his head.' He rubs the missing stub of finger against his chin.

'I could get money if the right people knew I was here.'

Fleet takes out a pipe, sucks on it. 'Who'd listen to the likes of me?' A thread of smoke twists up from the cup. 'Couldn't risk taking a letter out.'

He carries that smouldering pipe about, a little attention and it sparks to life. I must be like that, ready as a flame. 'Haslam's not good to his word. But Crowther he could be the man.'

'Him, do a good turn?' Fleet laughs, rubs his head. 'That's why they call you mad.'

'I think this chain, this one starboard. Seems a little stiff – like it might not pull back if needed. Maybe Crowther needs to take a look...'

Fleet picks up the bucket, is sure to leave but I need him still – what does he need from me? I tear the bread into little pieces, saving some to share with Davey...

Davey pads across the cell, crooked tail swaying.

I narrow my eyes.

He crosses back as a kitten, chasing after a spider. Here again as a kitten, rolling on his back. Another stretching in a beam of misplaced sunlight. More lying entwined on the cot, winding between my legs. Cats lying on the ground. Cats scratching at the wall. Cats scrabbling up the post, red flashes like prancing flames in the narrow beams of sunlight.

Davey is everywhere.

My hand drops. I didn't hurt Fleet's son, he hasn't hurt me: Fleet's a bartering man.

He fastens the lock. I lean towards the door, say, 'Haslam's always bringing Pomeroy sugar plums, he's not eaten the last lot – I'd have heard him cleansing.' I take a bit of bread. 'Bet your son, your wife, would love a sugar plum.'

Fleet spits on his pipe, tucks it away again. I can't see it, but I hear him go into Pomeroy's cell, hear him searching. Pomeroy squeaks like a mouse but he'll not speak to anyone but Haslam.

Fleet holds up the box, runs it against my bars. He rolls a plum into my cell. He walks away and maybe that's the last I'll hear of it. No deal, no Crowther. Not much of a loss. Listening to Pomeroy sucking on plums, heaving himself dry. I hold onto the wall, ease myself to standing. My legs throb.

The pulley trembles behind the wall, cogs scrape. *Not now, not yet, leave me loose a little longer.* I brace my arms against the edge of the cot, ready to resist. No yanking, no shortening of chains comes.

Fleet calls from the wall behind. 'Looks like some adjustments needed here. Crowther wouldn't want that to go unchecked.'

And if Crowther comes, what do I have to barter with him?

Need to know what he's thinking. Need to know what it would take for him to set me free.

I see him sitting in a chair. Swollen feet out of his boots, pushed under a desk. His fingers rub the lines of the drawing open in front of him. Lines turning to clouds as he worries at them. He pours himself more port, doesn't notice the dregs he has to chew down. His pen grows cold. His inkwell dries and cracks. He has no new contraptions. He has no new plans. Has nothing for the Board. He takes another drink.

And I notice that I've been writing, my hand moving through the air, writing and writing, but still thinking of Crowther. Crowther who is still sitting at his desk. Who hears Haslam scampering through the building, lining his nest. Who knows the younger man, Haslam, can keep this game going for longer. Who feels the cold, the emptiness of his bed, the emptiness of his belly, the emptiness of his gullet more than any man should. Who takes another drink. Who worries and worries where the next bottle will come from.

Crowther. Surely he'll not keep me waiting long.

I pick up the plum left by Fleet, sugar sticks to my fingers. I slide it into my mouth.

Gush of tropic sweetness – Ruth's lips – Ruth's breasts – tartness of stewed apples from the town's orchards – burn of rum – a burst of Paradise. It sinks me to my knees.

41

The night is held back by two lamps on the floor in the passage. Two giant rats are hunched up on the other side of the bars. My legs are wedged under the cot, can't kick out. If those monsters have a key I'm done for. They rise up, open the cell door but they're not rats, only Rodley and Crowther.

'Go chain him tight, Rodley. Check the cogs. I'll watch the movement from here.'

The pulley creaks, the chains crawl back against the cot. I go with them. I don't feel the chains anymore; holding them in my hand, shouldn't they weigh more? They're bone, my bone, part of me.

Wasn't I waiting for something?

Crowther stands by the cell door. It's dark. He leaves the lamp outside. His bloated shadow spills over me. The glow of the lamp caught in the sweaty reflection of his skin. Crowther puffs. His movement's heavy, skin rippling like he's filled with water. He stands in the puddle of light. An ocean of shadow between him and the cot.

He reaches into his coat, fumbling. Each movement threatens to topple him to the floor. It used to make the bile burn in my throat, to think when I was gone, those fingers would pick me apart. But perhaps it means less than nothing where I end.

Only wasn't there something I wanted?

Wake up, Norris. Wake up!

A speck of sugar crumbles on my fingertip; somewhere in that grain – the thing I must remember. A sugared plum – that taste...

Crowther calls, 'Test it again. The machine must hold.'

I keep my voice low. 'This machine will be hidden in cells, in cellars, no one will know your name. But Haslam's book, his name will be everywhere. He plots against you.'

'Ha!' Crowther frees a bottle, takes a slug. 'The Board, Haslam, we're all done for.' Spit dampens his white-streaked waistcoat.

I clench the edge of the cot. The sharp smell of gin brings back something – of a ship, of burning, of gunpowder, of shining...

He's not telling me, he's telling himself something, 'Won't be able to keep *them* out for long.'

I don't speak; it's not my answer he wants. But if he did, I'd ask, who is *Them*? It's familiar that word. Somewhere inside me a bell rings, change of watch is due. Them. Thought I was *Them*.

'I have something will bring you fame,' I say.

He holds onto the door. He thrusts his face closer, nose squashed against the bars. He sees straight through me, squinting, hoping I'll give him something. Am I a wall? A window? What... No, I shake my head. The surgeon has me mistaken. Not what but who... Who am I?

He sighs. 'Well, tell me this grand plan – what can it hurt?'

He waits. Wish he wouldn't stare. I rest against the stake, angling my head to get a glimpse of the stars. The stars – I plotted a course, to sail from these shores, to navigate myself to safe harbour, to Ruth. Fletcher is the one can give me safe passage beyond these walls.

I say, 'There's a man in here –'

'Yes, yes. Aren't there plenty of them?'

'I'll give you his name, but you'll never find him without me.'

'What's so special about this man that he'll make me famous?'

'Let me find him and you'll soon know.'

Crowther shakes his head. 'I need his name.'

Is that all it would have taken all those years before to get me out – his name? If they'd looked, they could have seen it scraped into the floor, the walls of this place. I laugh.

Coughing, dribbling, as if it's a last breath he takes. 'Laugh, would you?'

He throws the bottle against the wall. Pottery skitters across the floor. The smell of fresh, sharp spring rain. Too dark to see any stain. 'Tell me – or you'll never see your Ruth again.'

Ruth. The surgeon cuts open my soul, drags the chains through my heart.

He says, 'We've all heard you screaming that name.'

'And if I give you *his* name?'

'If I should be rewarded for finding this man, kept here at Bedlam. Then your case would be favourably reviewed. I could get you out.'

There is an out! After all these years, it could still be.

I'll say that name, let it be the surgeon's bounty. I lean towards the bars. 'Fletcher Christian.'

He slaps his leg, holds his guts, makes ohhing noises like he's trying to catch his breath. 'That's exactly what I need.'

He knows what that name means, what glory could be his. And what could be mine in return. He's shaking with the news, staggers, rests his head against the passage wall.

But he's laughing. Laughing and laughing until it becomes a sob. He wipes sweat from his eyes. 'They landed on Pitcairn months ago. The last man standing says it. All the papers say it. Christian is dead.'

It can't be true. 'There's a grave? A body?'

'No, no.' He shakes his head, wipes tears. 'Wouldn't that make it easier for Haslam to be rid of me – catch me debating with a mad man!'

The laughter still ripples through him. He stands a little straighter on the other side, back where he belongs, back where he knows who he is. The bars look so thin between his fat fists. 'In here you're safe from yourself, there's no release for you.'

I shout out, 'Fletcher Christian is here. I've seen him.'

Crowther wears chains can't be seen but will never break. See, they pull down his shoulders, bend his knees. He sinks under the weight of them.

A lamp goes with him. More darkness is all he leaves behind, and a scattering of pottery that crackles like eggshells as he walks away.

You'll not leave me stranded again, Fletcher.

The chains shake in my hands, I open my mouth to... I am not alone.

Crowther left something behind.

A stink of rotting seaweed comes, not lingering from Crowther, but from something darker which must have followed him in. It's not something to be hid from. It watches. A gaze so fierce the back of my neck burns.

It knows I'm awake. It can't be deceived. I roll on my side, lift myself onto my knees. Up at the top of the wall, starboard of the door, see it? Skulking in the darkest corner. It hangs from the bricks, wedged under the deckhead. Can't last there for long. Soon it will be too big to hide in corners.

Crowther walked it in like shit on his boots. I strain against the chains. The more I stare, the more clearly I see... Dark scales. Bayonet-sharp fin. Golden eyes.

Crowther's boots click-clop away. I don't bother to shout a warning. He'll meet the wicked creature soon enough, poor sod. The lurking beast will choose its moment to come out of the shadows – but for every battle, even in the thickest fog, there's a warning: the creak of a mainsail, the cough of a sailor, the distant flash of an eye glass. It'll give a signal too, it won't mean to but it will. I'll not turn my back on it.

I'll be ready.

People get out. They do.

The monster (that's surely what it is) might be resting now, but what if I fall asleep? What if it decides to take me tonight? There'll be no one to hear me scream.

Ruth? Will you be waiting?

She doesn't answer. I should wait by the crack in the wall just in case she appears.

If Fletcher really is – no – if it's so then so am I – no way out.

The monster will surely come for me now. It'll make me look into it, and I'll see all the world's horrors staring back, or maybe not the world's but just mine – and I'm scared that will be worse.

I have to know if Fletcher is here. If it wasn't him, what did I see? What have I been chasing? Fletcher hides in me, in my skin, blood, matted hair – was it just myself I saw?

The cell is still but not dark. The other lamp sits in the passage. I raise my eyes, head against the stake. The corner is empty. Why won't the monster show itself? I draw up my knees, hold my ankles. It could be anywhere. I hold my breath. Nothing moves. Why does the monster make me wait?

Only something does move.

There, I see it again. I hiss, 'Stay back.'

The monster stirs. It wrenches itself out of the stagnant corner of the cell. Slipping scales, rotten stench from the sea, gasping for air. A flash of scales, blinking golden eyes. The monster comes for me – a tasty treat of shit and bile. I cover my head with my arms.

The monster speaks, 'Fletcher Christian's a hero. Too clever to get killed by savages.'

I look up. Like sea spray the monster breaks apart, washing over the wall and floor. And Rodley is standing by the cell door.

'No grave. No body,' I say. 'I'm as dead as that. He was in the room next door, that year down below.'

'Those from that room were moved to the cellar.'

'I could find him.' But which promise do I keep? Paradise or hell for Fletcher?

'How?'

I hold up my hands. 'Unlock these chains. A lump in the straw and no one would miss me.'

Rodley squints, rubs his nose, but he doesn't walk away.

I say, 'Crowther unlocked me. Haslam should know that – if any trouble comes of this.'

Rodley nods. 'I'd be the man found Fletcher Christian. The man the navy couldn't capture.'

I nod.

He shakes his head. 'You're full of lies, he ain't here.'

'Wouldn't it be worth the look?'

Rodley squints, rubs a thumb in his eye. 'Has to be something sure in it for me.'

I try to think of what I have. Nothing but this cap, this gown. I pull at it, the gown tears about my legs.

Rodley raises the lamp. 'Gold.'

On the floor at my feet lies my collection of teeth, crowned with gold, sparkling in the light. They were the first to fall out, before Rodley carved his own share.

He takes out his keys, comes into the cell. He bends down scoops the teeth into his hand. But he will take them and leave, leave me here.

'If you don't take me to the cellar I'll die, but that won't be the end of me – I'll haunt you, Rodley. You'll curse the day you betrayed me. Think Hooke's coin was tainted? That's nothing to the hell I'll bring down on you.'

The gold glows under his chin; he bounces them for weight.

I whisper, 'You'll be the man captured Fletcher Christian.'

Rodley drops the teeth into his pocket. But he doesn't leave, he unlocks the chains about my wrists, my ankles, my guts, my neck.

He beckons me into the passage. 'What did I do but fall victim to a violent incurable? I'll be a hero either way.'

I take a step. My legs shake, I balance against the cot. No blow comes. No laughter. He presses the stick into my chest, moves me against the passage wall. 'Try anything – I'll kill you,' he says but he only has one hand on the stick.

He picks up the lamp with the other. Another prod. He thinks

I'm broken: nothing but a thin-legged, weak-armed, droop-necked creature. And I think he's right.

Pomeroy sleeps in his cell, an embroidered blanket covering him. This is a dead end. Rodley's walking me into nothing. But something winks in the light. A keyhole. A door.

42

Into the guts of Bedlam we go, down steps, worming through passages. Light from the lamp leads the way as if we are an old fireship on course to collide, to burn everything down. Legs shake, press a hand to the wall, rough rubbing brick. I'm out of the cell, no matter what happens now I made it out.

How many years? Three, eight, twelve? A lifetime? Out.

Bedlam grows and grows. The boards stretch like giant oaks come back to life. The bricks big as battle ships. Storm's running along the sides out there, battering to get in.

Fletcher?

Paradise could have been ours, James.

I'd run if I could, if this broken down hull of a body would let me. What if this turn leads only to another corner and another? Sailing full circle back to the cell and the chain and the stake. What if there's no getting free?

What's waiting down here, Fletcher?

Nobody.

Rodley holds the light higher. Not enough to see where I tread. Thump and bang of ankles and elbows. The years in chains has set my body off kilter. The lamp warms the back of my neck, swinging over my shoulder. Passage narrows, doors, bars. More doors. More bars. Blackness floods cells. Hold that light steady. Let me get sight of him I want.

Paradise or hell for you? But is it you, Fletcher?

Run my knuckles along bars. Thud thud thud. Heads look up, shrink away again.

Men. Men everywhere, but not the one I seek. All the faces look like mine. The cries, the screams – could be my voice.

'Show yourself,' I shout.

No one hears me. Can't hear myself. Storm is here. Another cell. Another cell. All look the same inside and out.

We are rats. Crawling, screeching. Tail to teeth. Blood and fur. Trapped.

Don't cast anchor yet. Keep sailing onwards.

Light haloes another cell. Men lying like fallen bricks. Bedlam has toppled. This here, all that's left.

I grab the lamp, it burns, but there, there in the corner – a heap of rags on the ground. Rodley snatches the lamp back, it swings. Shadows like masts, cast by light falling through the bars. Feet and legs. Darkness again.

I grip the door. 'Here.'

Rodley holds his nose, pushes me aside, peers through the bars. Looks where I point. 'That's him? Ain't much left.'

But something about that slumped creature is familiar. I shake the handle.

'This was a waste.' Rodley jangles the teeth in his hands, jumps them into his pocket. 'Look if you must.'

Rodley unlocks the door, shoves me in. He kicks it shut again, checks it is locked by shaking the bars. 'Hurry. I'm due at the Rose and Crown.'

Need to see what's in that bundle. Men stand shoulder to shoulder, trying to get at the door. Men. Swarming, round and round, glistening of their eyes: a churning shoal of fish. No room to pass. No space to tell arm from arm, leg from leg. Limbs locked together. Press my shoulder forward, take a step. Some push back. Rolled against the wall. Dig nails into the soft bricks, dragged deeper in. Cell, chains – go back there. Not used to the touch, the stink of these savages, these all-the-sames.

Shadows give no corners to the place, all huddle in a circle of light from Rodley's lantern at the door. Down in the depths it lies.

Prod the bundle with a thumb, it doesn't move. Dig in a little deeper. There is something delicate, jangling to the touch. Snatch hand away. Grey cloth sticks to it like porridge. An arm hangs out of the winding sheet. Drop to knees.

Peel back the top of the cloth. So thin and small. Fletcher was tall, if bent a little at the knee. Fletcher was dusky. The hair is white as if the body is dipped in snow. The nose, delicate chin, and curled ears are those of a boy. Eyes closed, mouth open... the face. From a time above, from a time when there were only the days to count – how many since arriving here?

The body flinches, a pursing of the lips. Did he hear from beyond? Returning him from the dead?

'Parrot Boy.'

The lips gape again. Still a boy despite the lined face, the grey hair. Not dead but not living. They're already drained him, laid him out for that butcher Crowther.

Lift his chin. 'Take another breath. Beat this.' Light as a cup, Parrot Boy's head rests in lap. His eyelids flutter but don't open. Skin grey, so thin that the veins beneath look like blue worms.

'Is anyone waiting for you?' Lower ear to his mouth. Ragged

breathing, nothing more, nothing that can be told. 'Bet there's a mother, one loves you as her boy – you'll always be her boy.' Smooth the thinning hair back from his brow.

Pat his chest. Death tugs. Parrot Boy takes a rattling breath.

Whisper, 'Keep fighting.'

Keep fighting?

What have you been fighting, James? We could have been happy, us and the baby, didn't have to leave the sea, just return to us. You cast off, James, without another thought – others I'd have expected –

Ruth? He searched, he did.

Meant to kill me, I heard. You never loved me, James.

He was wrong, Ruth, was hisself he wanted to hurt. And Fletcher –

He mentions me, left me too didn't you, James? I had to take the Bounty, you weren't there to help me –

Fletcher, he never stopped searching for you.

Why did you save me, James? Why did you promise me something you never meant to give? Paradise –

He remembers it still, Fletcher. You were a drowning man then, you always were. He was too coward to go down with you.

He's glad his mother never lived to see him brought so low. Shit and dirt of this, not this place, this him.

I see you son, your father here, and I see you for your mother too.

How will she know him from Heaven, so far far far down below, father?

The Lord makes us all in his image, my boy. One day I hope you'll see the joy in what you are, not only the longing for what you could be.

I needed you / I needed you / I needed you –

Don't all speak at once.

Parrot Boy grabs my hand, holds me.

It strikes me now, the smallness, of Parrot Boy – small head, small hands. My mother, father, William, Fletcher, Ruth – I wanted them to all be more than they were – hated them for their smallness, their failings. But I should have been, if not a hero, a good, true man. I let them down. The weakness was all mine.

Sometimes it's the promises we break; sometimes it's the promises break us.

The weakness is mine.

Do you hear that Fletcher? Do you hear that Ruth? Do you hear it? I did this.

'Wait for your mother, Parrot Boy, she'll come.' I lift him under the arms, hold him about the chest. 'I'll not let them take your living soul.'

I scoop up a handful of straw from the floor, push it around Parrot Boy's thin legs, the knees swollen up like bowls. 'That'll keep you warm.'

His head rests against my chest. If he should leave this cage, I hope he has wings at last, bright yellow and orange feathers, and sharp claws to protect himself from those who'd hope to net him.

I squeeze his hand. I squeeze his hand again – like the way he repeated everything. Can everything be repeated? A sea mist rolls up from the Thames, slithering through the mud and stone floor. Can everything be repeated?

I try to bat the haze away from my head, but it slides into my mouth and nose. There's a time I'd have welcomed it, knew it meant a new voyage is coming, that sails and masts would soon be rising above me. Only now I know it comes to torment me with a taste of all I can't have.

I hope Fletcher is far from here. I hope Ruth is loved.

The mist joins with the winding sheet, drapes itself about us, swirls around the cell. I'm not the only one longs to be free. But the mist is too thick, it will blanket the sky.

I stand up, shout, 'Leave the boy and take me. I'm ready.'

Something steps out of the gloom. Tall, thick-limbed. 'Fletcher?'

Hands seize me about the throat. It is the soldier, how long has he been awake? His nose is cracked in on itself, his eye droops. I did that. But the Pisser sees me with his one good eye. He flings me to the wall.

I drop. Chomping air. The soldier shakes me from myself.

My eyes close. I'm ready.

My chin tips up, back bent. Upturned, I glimpse the heavens.

Stars shine brightest of all at sea.

Celestial navigation. Onboard we live by it. Each sailing a journey through waves of light, sparks of brightness white hot as shot. I swear I hear the stars hiss; see them steam in the distance where the sky slips into the sea. It is my favourite watch, the early hours – long after the first bright surge of the Dog Star, hours before the sun bleeds red.

Sea

Waves

Even a storm. Give me a storm! What I wouldn't give for the mad mad work of rigging, sails, sloshing, battening down, wet ropes, salt-slapped faces...

In the distance, Rodley calls, but I'm nearly overboard. Something stands in my way. It has me about the neck. Meat breath. Rodley beats him with a stick.

I am back to that day with the soldier in the yard. All that happened in the cell, to the man tied to the stake, has not happened yet.

The soldier digs his nails into the sores on my neck – sweet feeling. I shut my eyes again. Press harder, man.

Inside, Ruth. That's where I should stay.

I feel the soft brush of Ruth's hand on my shoulder. She holds me still.

It is beautiful inside, isn't it Ruth?

His grip tightens. Gasping. My knees give. No air. Let it bring a deeper darkness, one from which there's no waking.

43

The stars are back, each in its own hanging.

I'm up on deck. A cool breath from the east lifts the hair on my head. A man of the watch stands ahead of me on the weather deck. The quartermaster has the wheel, navigating the ship through safe waters. Sextant raised, he plots a course for us between the moon and the stars. Celestial bodies tipping and tilting – this way, follow me, they sing. Their night-time brilliance allows the compass rose to bloom in its cabinet by the wheel.

Venus, Mars, Polaris, names as sweet and soft in the mouth as honey. I hold onto the deck rail, tilting out into the darkness. Their reflections in the water, bright enough to light up the ocean, make shadows of us all.

The bell rings. I look up. I see his face. The moon paints him blue as fresh milk. Fletcher stands on the poop deck. I reach the ladder, but my feet are thick like clay. I heave myself higher, hands pulling myself up onto the deck. I roll over, exhausted. He stands just out of reach.

Fletcher holds a chart in front of him, stretched tight. He frowns, nose screwed, eyes squinting. Is he angry or afraid? I'm too low down to tell. Pull myself up onto my knees. I want to see where he leads us. I reach out, nearly have the edge of Fletcher's cloak but he steps away, rolls up the chart.

He calls to the first mate, the watch bell drowns him out. He signals, with the waving of his arms, for the boat to hold course. I drag myself to standing, neck sore, knees shaking. Where are we heading? I whistle to get the first mate's attention. He's gone.

We two are the only ones aboard.

Who's at the wheel?

The ship steers herself. We go too fast. I tumble back to the quarterdeck, roll up against the wheel. Alongside, a crest of luminous waves sends splashes across the bowsprit, over the ship. Fletcher jumps, ducks away from the cold spray. I am nearly there, nearly have the wheel.

The sky ripens to deep purple. We're hastening towards dawn. Fletcher waves and waves, arms crashing into each other like a mainsail left unfurled in a storm. I lean into the wind. Clouds and waves passing faster than they ever have before. Too many knots to keep a steady course. The bell is blown from its hanging. The ringing stops.

Fletcher shouts, 'Bear onward.'

But there is no one else on watch to hear. The waves swell. I try to hold onto the wheel. It spins and spins.

No ship has ever travelled so fast.

'Paradise is near,' he shouts.

I turn to face him. Fletcher grips his hands together. The spray thickens into a sea mist. It snags on the rigging, lifts the corners of our coats, slaps at our backs. The wind tries to get under my feet, tip me into the sea. I look up, searching for a still point, for balance. We are spinning about the stars, the light that turns the world.

Only they aren't stars. The more I stare the more clearly I see – we are turning over, rolling like a whale. The smasher guns are uncapped, grapeshot spills. It darkens the deck like a cloud of flies but it can't block out the light for long. The brightness is algae, shining through the deep like being suspended in amber. We are upside down. I let go of the rail but the weight of water holds me. The ship rights itself but we are deep under the sea.

The water, soft as a caress, trails through my hair, across my skin. Turn my hands over – clean and shining. The algae stick to my breeches, my shirt and coat. Fletcher is furred too. It makes us glow, blurring us until we are spilling out of our edges. Nothing is as it was. The waves are high above, they can't touch us. The sails are carried on by the tide, leaving a golden trail behind.

Fletcher still shouts but water deadens the words. He flaps his arms, claws at his mouth. He fights it. Small things surface, the bottles, the shoes, the strips of cloth, but the sea doesn't like to give up men, clasps them tighter than any lover. I could tell him that but his own fear deafens him. He already thinks himself a drowned man. His arms flail, his coat flaps. And I'm glad not to see the horror on his face. Such panic can sink a whole crew.

This turning upside down of everything is a shock to him, and that's a shock to me. Anything can happen, doesn't he know that? If he's not careful, he'll tip himself overboard. Could I save him? What am I? Less than seaweed, less than –

'You are my starlight, James Norris.'

Ruth.

I spin around, the water wraps me up in my clothes like a winding sheet. She stands at the wheel. 'And you mine, Ruth.'

Her hair like a fine silk ensign streams behind her. She has her own glorious wake. I glide towards her – have only to think it and it happens. We stand together. She puts her hands on top of mine. We guide the ship.

I rest my chin on the crown of her head. 'I've been hunting inside for you, Ruth.'

She points ahead. 'Out there, look.'

I hold a hand up to my eyes, inspect the horizon. She lifts her head to tell me something. Her smile fades, her neck twisted. She opens her mouth to call a warning. No words come out. She pulls away from me. The wheel spins again.

We face each other. Her mouth still open, lips drawn back. She drops to her knees. Her back curved, head low. I crouch in front of her. There is no sound, just bubbles, before a splash of water, a small length of dark green seaweed pokes out of her mouth.

Her head snaps back, her eyes roll. Something is coming. It shows in her fluttering eyelids and clawed fingers. She's spitting, heaving. It spews out of her: blubber, skin, bone, pieces of rag.

Putrid stink of rotting fish, uncovered graves. I fall backwards, hands down. Between coughing spews, she pants. But the bubbles, the filth begins to slide together. Bone on skin, blubber on rag, blubber, bone, shell, stones. An ancient, terrible stench.

It sloshes towards my boots. I scuttle away like a crab, tripping over laid out rigging lines. Ruth wipes her hand across her mouth, holds onto the wheel and raises herself. She has nothing more to give. She looks down on me, calls out, 'Go back, go back...' The rest lost in choking gasps.

What does she mean – go somewhere, or go away?

The soupy mass is still collecting itself together, growing, glowing in the algae light. I drag myself away. My back hits the cabin door. I must retreat or be swallowed down.

Clouds of fish begin to form above us, one breaks away from the shoal, darts onto the deck, nipping, nibbling at the growing carcass. Glinting scales, flicking tails, golden eyes – more come to feast. Mackerel. Flying through the water, slapping along the deck.

I can't see Ruth. Can't see Fletcher.

The door gives. I tumble into the cool gloom of the Captain's cabin. I kick the door shut. I'm a coward to leave Ruth again, though she made me do it. Go back? Go somewhere...

I run my hand over the maps and charts spread on the Captain's table. A lamp hangs from the middle of the room. There must be a way, a passage to plot through all these seas. I push my finger along the blue and green-inked lines.

Here be monsters, uncharted waters everywhere.

Footsteps creak outside the cabin. I snatch my hand away. I'll be for it if I'm caught in here. They'll hang me for a mutineer.

I back away from the door, take the ladder to the main deck.

Light shines out from under the quartermaster of provisions store. I put my eye to the keyhole.

Fletcher stands against the wall. He must have come down from another deck. What does he look at in his hands? What do those charts show? Why does he stare, shake his head? I squeeze my face to the door, eye right up against the keyhole.

He blocks my view. He leans over, nose touching the chart. I press my body against the door, fingers groping at the hole, clearing the muck. I must see what he sees. Maybe Fletcher knows the way.

Go back. Go back.

44

There's a voice, low and wordless like the beat of water against a hull. Warmth wraps around me, stretches out my limbs. Keep me safe, feed me, please. A brush of a hand. Hold me. I'll stay here with you.

But there's still a waking to come.

I'm not dead.

My body twitches as it does after each sleep, but the chains don't snap me back. I stretch my legs. Pain pushes a groan out of my hollow body.

I try to open my eyes. A burning yellow brightness like the sun has broken itself before me. I pull the blanket over my head. A blanket. Wool tickles my lips. Never had a blanket before. It is warm as a... as a blanket. I roll myself in it.

I hear other things: the splash of water as the bucket is filled, the slosh of something ladled into a bowl. My throat is too dry to get out any words. But moisture dampens my lips. Steam.

I roll onto my back, stick my tongue to the blanket, taste the air. Meaty soup and warm bread. I'd snatch for them but I don't want to put my hand through this vision. I'll stay safe under here.

My bones settle, all knots and corners like I might break through what skin I have left.

The pattern of yellow light, shining through the blanket's weave, begins to fade. Fleet's boots wait by the bars of the cell, the toes cracked, the eyelets ripped, the leather rotting about him.

He whispers, 'Rodley with his tales of chasing you through the cellar and him plucking Parrot Boy from death's jaw.'

The boy's alive at least.

'Believe it?' He shrugs. 'We're in Bedlam, aren't we?'

Fleet talks but there's no anger in his words. 'I promise help is coming. Just stay awake. I'll fetch more soup.'

45

Something is coming.

Last week a man knocked at the gates of Bedlam and was turned away. The bricks hum with tales of it.

The next day, or a next day but I'm not sure of which, there is another knock. I don't hear it. I hear of it.

Now they're coming for me.

Rodley throws the keys at Fleet. 'I'm not doing it.' He points. The keys lie on the ground between them. 'Ain't you his mate?'

Fleet licks his lips, sniffs. 'Give them here. Can't put up with you crying like a baby.'

Rodley bends down, hands them over. 'We'll all be out on the street singing Bedlam ballads. Or maybes it's not our skin the government is after.'

Fleet unlocks the door. 'Don't be so sure, that Haslam's slippery as a shitting eel.'

Footsteps sound along the passage. Fleet and Rodley shift a little closer together, trying to make themselves bigger, to fool the thing heading their way.

Haslam's voice echoes off walls. 'I want it noted that you entered these rooms –'

'Rooms!' A new voice rises in Bedlam, 'Call them what they are, Mr Haslam. Cells. Cells each and everyone.'

'Now, aren't we all gentlemen here.' Another voice I've not heard before.

'No, we aren't.' Haslam spits out the words. 'This floor is for the most violent and deranged. I don't advise you to enter, Mr Wakefield.'

'I don't suppose you do. I've seen nothing but ill treatment and neglect.'

They are coming, coming but I don't know what for. Perhaps there is nothing left for me to know. I will lie down and sleep, sleep for the rest of days.

The voices are closer now. *Monster, my eyes are closed against you*. Shapes glide out there. Someone opens the bars. Must have opened every door and window in the place. Light creeps in. Put an arm over my eyes, but it won't reach, push my fingers against my eyebrows instead.

'He took Fleet's finger off,' Rodley whines

Fleet digs him in the ribs. They jostle.

'Never mind all that,' Haslam snaps. 'It is not safe to enter, Mr Wakefield.'

'Mr Haslam, I'm not here to do as you bid,' the new voice says.

They are inside.

They are close to the cot.

'I'm Edward Wakefield, this is MP –'

'Dear God, Wakefield. He's chained to a pole.'

'What instrument of torture is this?' Wakefield's voice rises and falls as he speaks, has yet to be flattened by Bedlam.

The other man clucks like a hen, 'Chained by the neck. This

will not do, not at all, Mr Haslam. I must insist you answer Mr Wakefield's question. What is the reason for this?'

Haslam sighs. 'I can give no reason for the contrivance at all, not having contrived it.'

'This is Surgeon Crowther's doing then?'

Haslam waits before answering. 'You could ask him but you shan't get any clear answer, not until the inn opens.' His words slither like a snake.

But this new man Wakefield is fast on his feet. 'You let your life preach. Be careful, Mr Haslam – you mark yourself out as the only man with sense in Bethlem.'

Rodley puffs up. 'Mr Haslam do run this place. All his hard –'

Haslam thumps the ledger on Rodley's shoulder, silencing him. The force of the blow pops his collar. Rodley scrabbles for it on the floor.

The older man paces the end of the cell, tutting to himself. 'How long does such punishment last?'

Haslam replies, 'I couldn't say.'

Mr Wakefield says, 'Look in that ledger you are so attached to.'

A flicking sound of skin on leather. Haslam says, 'The ledger tells me he was admitted in 1800. Incurables in 1801. So, he's been with us for over fourteen years.' Turning pages. Haslam coughs.

Mr Wakefield snaps, 'These chains, how long has the man been restrained like this?'

'Counting forward, well – that's a little smudged... Ten.'

Mr Wakefield pushes out each word, 'Days? Weeks?'

Haslam coughs again. 'Years.'

'Ten years!'

Silence. Have they gone?

Ten years in these chains. The years before these chains, were there four of them? It has sailed by. It has felt like the longest lifetime ever lived.

'And I suppose he blackened his own eyes, tore open his own skin, with these chains on him.' So close, there is breath on my hands. Mr Wakefield is before me. 'What is your name, sir?'

My name? No words fall out of my cracked lips. I tug at the chain about my neck. Their light is too bright. Can't look. Press my hands harder into my eyes.

'I'm Edward Wakefield. Can you tell me your name?'

Who am I?

I am a sea chest of thoughts and memories, fear and longing, rats and fleas, and monsters.

I am monsters – too many to count.

46

But I am also this:

I am twelve when I first slip free of myself, the self that I know.

'Don't leave the yard,' my stepmother calls from the cottage. 'Keep your lugs open for the little'uns.'

We hear the front door close, my brother and me. He turns his head; I rap him on the knuckles.

I laugh as he sucks his fingers. 'Another win for me.'

I'm supposed to be chopping wood, but I got so bored it hurt. Tormenting William seemed like more fun. Now I'm bored of that too. I lie on top of the woodpile. There aren't many trees left on the lane, just the cherry in the ironmonger's yard next door. The leaves are ripening, getting set to fall, but the sun still shines. Newcomers go on about the beauty of a place where summer never ends. The first fall of snow freezes their mouths. They call it New England. I should like to see the old England one day.

I've never seen much of anything. I spit out a leaf that's landed on my face, jump down from the pile. I stand at the back gate.

'We're not allowed to leave the yard,' my brother whines, sore hand pressed between his thighs.

'She's your mother but not mine,' I answer, one leg dangling over the brace.

There are Indian arrowheads out on the other side of the orchards and I mean to get me some. I won't spend the rest of my life shut away in this cottage, this yard, this town. Maybe I'll go to sea, see things folks in this stupid stinking place couldn't even imagine (most of them too scared by their own sea crossing to even fish the harbour). They landed in Boston and took root quicker than bindweed – but not me, I've places to be.

I climb over the rail. And standing in the lane it feels like my arms, my legs, my head, can all move at last.

My brother sticks his chin on top of the stile. 'The twins are sleeping.'

'Better that than screaming. Stay with the babies if you want.'

William is ten but small and thin for his age. He's always got the shits. He likes to think himself big though. He scratches his backside.

I wave, take the back path away from the row of cottages. I know he won't be far behind. I want him to follow, seems no point doing something daring if no one sees it. Before I pass the privy, I hear him sneezing behind me, puffing and holding his nose against the dark slimy pit which leaks black mud. He spends so much time in there it's a wonder he's not used to it.

He trots to catch up, tugs at my shirt sleeve. 'Where we going?'

I keep walking.

Don't feel like telling him about the arrowheads, he'll only blurt it out to any fool we meet on the way. No one's supposed to go out past the fences.

He farts, tries to cup it and stick it under my nose but I shove him into the dust.

William claps dirt off his hands, turns his head towards the cottage. 'Is that crying?'

'Go back if you're scared. That's where I'm going.' I point out past the lane, and the Meeting House.

'Just to the orchards?'

I nod. He looks back again, then over to the treetops, puts his head down and follows me. We crawl under the Meeting House windows, in case our father is in there preaching on Paradise. Revelation is his favourite –'And I saw a new heaven and a new earth: for the first heaven and the first earth were passed away; and there was no more sea.'

We're out of the town. We've sneaked around One Eyed Jane's garden full of withered lupins. We're on the edge of it all now. The mud isn't trampled into ruts here. Loose dust dances about our feet. The apple fair has been and gone. No one else will be out this way.

Through the orchard we go. Leaves rustling, seeming on fire, so much red, gold, and yellow flickering above our heads. But the low outline of the fence juts up between the twisted tree trunks. We're getting close. I tell myself it's only fencing.

I put my hands on the top pole. Long grass sways on the other side, sweeping low towards the giant trees of the forest. There's nothing new about this land. It is ancient and endless. Our father says we're settlers which sounds to me like we're only passing through. There's a rope about my waist tethers me to England. Though I've never been, it's my Mother Country, and where my mother's life began. I'm not meant to be out there on the other side. That's where she went, paddling along the creek, out into the pool of cool water.

The blackness of the trees, taller than anything in the orchard, anything I've ever seen, it draws me. I lean over the fence. The riverbed and the arrows are waiting for me just on the other side of the tall trees. I hear the water. I hear something...

'Let's go back.' My brother's voice wavers like the leaves.

'You're a pup.'

He stands too close, making my skin itchy. He whispers, 'There's savages out there.'

I step away from him. 'Think this fence would stop them?'

'Don't go.' His pale eyes are just like my father's but not like mine. He's only half a brother, half a little streak of piss – why would I listen to him?

They're cowards all of them, too afraid to do nothing. I pick up a rotten apple, throw it at his head. He ducks but it hits his shoulder, splattering dark juice and flecks of red skin. He'll take a whipping for that mess.

He doesn't seem to notice, pushes his fists into his gut. 'I've got a bad bad feeling.'

And now he's said it, I feel it too, deep inside like a rumbling river running through me. If you fall in a river everyone knows you let it take you, don't fight the current, don't struggle for a hanging root, or branch. Float, wherever it takes you, go with the river. Go with the river. I put both hands on the fence.

'If you're going, you'll need a look out.' My brother scampers to the closest tree. Apples stripped off, branches pointing straight out. He climbs it like a ladder.

When it happens I'm standing, head tilted, hands on hips, back to him, and the apple tree. My brother treads on a rotten branch, can't take his weight. It snaps. A crack like rifle fire.

'William!' I cry out, try to turn. But I'm not there on the edge of the orchard anymore, I'm not even me.

I'm with my mother. A fire burns in the hearth, snow piles against the window. A draught swims through the room like fish following their own course. I rest against my mother's shoulder; she sits in a low rocking chair. The wind outside sounds high and sharp like crying. My mother strains to look up at me but the whiteness of the snow behind me is blinding. I lower my face but she still can't see me, rubbing her eyes, reaching to find my hand. She's staring at something behind me. I turn around.

And I'm back in the orchard. My brother's falling.

I'm running to the tree, arms out.

He smacks into the scratchy leaves, squashing open rotting windfall, scattering the last of the wasps. I crouch beside him. His head snapped back. Eyes open. He doesn't see me. He doesn't move.

He's far beyond the yard, beyond the orchard, the forest, the river. He's somewhere I can't follow. I bend down, try to lift him under the arms. He's heavier than he ever looked, a weight I can't hold. He slips from my grip back into the leaves. But all I can think is that I've lost my mother again, the horrible boiling guilt that I should have stayed with her not run to him. Now, I'm left with nothing.

His arm flops from my grip. My brother isn't there.

I've seen it happen on ships, the fall – arms unfurling like wings, shirt fluttering like feathers. Before they hit the deck or masts – wood and iron cracking them open like an egg – it sounds like a flock of gulls coming into land – there's a quivering moment when hope makes you think all will be well. The dull thud like a wet axe into a rotten tree breaks the childish dream. Bones split from skin, blood bursting – knocked clean out of themselves.

But if you're quick you can swallow down their last breath, capture their soul between your cupped hands like a fallen chick, and return it to loved ones waiting on land.

Or you can hold out your arms – try to catch them.

Perhaps I never should have caught Fletcher, should have let him feel the crack of a fall back then when he was young enough to heal. Saving him didn't save my brother. Floating in the dark Atlantic Ocean, waiting to be missed by the change of watch. I never should have promised Fletcher anything. Paradise wasn't mine to give. Then on The Bounty, when he needed help again, when it all came tumbling down – where was I?

I wasn't there to save him.

47

I am falling
falling
falling
falling
for so long now, perhaps I'm stuck, perhaps I'll never land

My mother rocks in her chair   My brother flies   Ruth kisses my fingers   My father's voice   Smell of fermenting apples, deep rivers   Ruth stands in the mud, tells me I'm a fool   The scratch of corn stalks in my palm   Blood, splash of landing mackerel   Ruth kisses my fingers   Brother soars   Rainbow flashes of fish scales   Corn stalks and mud   Kisses   Ruth   Rivers run   My father's voice

Don't fight it

48

'William,' I whisper, chest rising, nostrils flaring. Not quite right but as close to the ground as I'm able to get in this moment.

'The man doesn't have his senses – obviously.' Haslam reads from the ledger as if he's never met me either. 'It's written here as James Norris.'

No, not that name. That man is gone.

III

BEATING WINDWARD

49

London, 1815

That was that and this is this and this is what I want.

Maybe I've spent my life beating windward, learning and living the hard way. I've been out of that cell for three weeks. Every journey has a purpose. Now here I am.

Here is a window, with glass not bars. Here is a bed with a blanket, a straw-plumped pillow. Here is a bucket and cloth. The water is changed each day, and it's just for washing. Here's a bright blue pitcher of water to drink. Here's a shelf, a cupboard, two chairs. Between me and the window is a table. My fingers slide over the worn wood, dips and grooves. Someone has tried to plane away the carvings, but with my eyes closed I feel the shape of letters. A *T*, a *B* or *E*. It could mean anything, but for me it's become a message of hope.

Light falls through the window, still smeared with London filth, but I can see the sky, the thick clouds. At night, from the bed, I see clear up to the stars.

The newness of *here* swirls me through the days.

Here life is as I'd forgotten it could be.

No chains, no stake, to hold me. I walk around the table to

sit by the window. I stretch out my legs, fold my arms behind my head. The ceiling is mapped with a thousand tiny cracks, each one is a new path, a fresh journey to take. But I always come back for food. I'm hungry, not for the soups and cheese and meat pies but for the company. Twice a day, with bread. I might begin to think myself royalty. And like royalty I'll change laws. Well, not really me – for that I must thank Mr Wakefield, my friend the Quaker.

Here's a knock at the door. I sit up. I've already had food today, the bowl sits on the table. Another knock. I know who it must be. I get up, go past the window. The trees, the grass (patchy this time of year but still green) bright enough to half imagine it is the sea. There is an order to this room, this new life, that is familiar and comforting to me.

'Hello,' I call out. I don't know what would happen if I didn't answer, if it would all go away: the visitors, the food, the bed, the table and chairs.

The door opens.

'Mr Wakefield, have a seat.' I dust it with the back of my hand.

My friend the Quaker comes when he can. He lays a newspaper on the shelf by the door, as he usually does. He brings them to help me keep the date clear in my head. For the time there is a clock. Tick tick tick on the shelf, loud in my ear. I stand to attention.

'Good morning, Marine Norris.' As easy as roll call, and he promoted me. I have him to thank for my freedom.

We move the spindly chairs towards the window as we always do. We sit facing the street, the blue streaks of sky run along the rooftops opposite. He fits his hat and cloak on the back of the chair.

He folds his hands in his lap. He often sits this way and I wonder if he is saying his prayers, if I might be in them?

He smiles. 'Is the room still to your liking?'

'I shouldn't like anywhere better.' Free of them and all that. 'Haslam must come and see me – see how I fare without him – when I'm fully well you could fetch him.'

He nods, presses his hands tighter together. 'I pray for your health.'

'Being here betters me no end.'

A starling flutters down on the sill, presses its feathers to the window, spreading like frost on the glass. I reach over, gently span my fingers on the window, wider than the feathers.

'God's blessing.' He releases his hands; they come to settle on his legs.

I nod and bow my head a little. I am grateful of course and if he puts all of it at God's feet, that's where I'll give my respect, if he wants it.

Outside the starling chatters to his mate. A dog barks for his master. We're all seeking companionship. I tap the glass, set the bird into flight. Mr Wakefield flinches; usually he sits so still that he could be taken for a statue, but today his hands flap, he taps a foot. He glances at the shelf then sits forward, scraping his chair a little closer to mine. He says, 'Should you like to go outside?'

I shrug. 'Soon.'

'When you're feeling stronger?'

I nod, tilt my head to catch the sun like the weeds sprouting from the windowsill. Sympathy is sweet as honey in rum, it does things to you: smoothes the edges, softens the daylight – you can drink down oblivion. If I wasn't a marine a tear might spring in my eye. He has nothing to gain but still he helps me. Mr Wakefield stretches out his feet, it's probably the only rest he'll have all day – he's a busy man but one happy with silence. Perhaps that's why I like his visits. He doesn't try to speak all the time, filling peace with questions and statements. He's the sort of man who would make an excellent castaway mate. The silence stretches between us – clouds glide, birds swoop, someone moves a chair on the other side of the wall, a cartwheel clicks on the cobbles outside – we're swaddled together like infant and mother.

I'd all but given up hope I'd make it out of that cell alive. Lost in the cracks and crevices, the straw and the filth. No compass to guide me... but that's not true. Ruth, there was always Ruth.

I take myself to stand by the window. White clover in the grass, red apples on the cart, a pretty skirt passing by, all these things remind me of Ruth. I shift from foot to foot. I feel something, a throb in my balls. That's something after being numb down there for... for however long it was. Maybe I'm not to be crippled forever. I can get back all those bits of myself I thought were gone.

Ruth won't find me in this new place. I never meant to make her stay, to keep her caged with me in that hole. I'm sure I still have it in me to get free. Although, God's seen the cruelty in me – my family all gone – and my Ruth – I must find her. I'd feel if she isn't still walking among the living. But if she should die before I reach her... that would be a voyage I could never take, to meet her in that better place.

A small cough brings me back to the room. Mr Wakefield says, 'Shall I get some tea brought up?' He always has a care for others.

'Water's enough for me,' I say.

That is the truth. The fresh stone taste of it, like I'm swallowing the blue of the jug. I could drink it all day but I wouldn't want someone having to run up and down stairs for me, so I ration it.

I fetch two cups, pour out more for Mr Wakefield. It gives me pleasure to be able to offer him something.

'God's blessing,' he says, smiling at the cup.

He takes a sip or two. I stop myself from gulping it down.

'Am I the only one to be set free?'

'Conditions are being improved for everyone,' he says.

It is something a reformer would say, but then that's what he is.

'What made you knock at Bedlam?'

He grips the cup; an angry man might have cracked the pottery, but his hand trembles as he sets it down. 'I heard rumours – terrible things.'

'Most cross to the other side of the street.'

He smiles, wags a finger at me. 'I see what you do, Marine Norris.'

I fold my arms over my chest. 'Why shouldn't I make a Good Samaritan of you?'

'My motives were anger and fear.' He hangs his head, rubs the back of his neck. 'I know what such places can do.'

Though he has turned his face aside, I see the burn of shame on his cheeks. Mine is not the only pain in this beautiful new room. 'Who did you lose?'

'My mother was locked away,' he says truthfully when most men would have found time to spin a lie.

'We blame ourselves but boys can't save their mothers, no matter how much we try.'

He nods. 'You're a thoughtful man, Marine Norris.'

If I really was such a man, I'd correct him, tell him of my many un-thoughtful thoughts. But I suppose he must mean that a man can think when he is seen as a man and not as an animal.

He glances back to the shelf. Usually he places the paper on the table or the bed, happy to discuss something he's read, but not today. There must be something he needs from me, some way of helping him – a man shouldn't leave his debts unpaid.

'If you wish me to speak with more Parliament men – if you think it will help others –'

'No, you'll have your peace. Parliament sits soon.'

The man's a true reformer, he'll put them all back on course – until the next storm. The clock clicks into a new hour. He gets ready to leave, coat, hat; he sets everything in place. I see him to the door.

Some business keeps him in the room. He turns away from me, places his hand on the newspaper rolled up on the shelf. 'If you wish to see it...' He taps the paper. 'Or I can remove it.'

He makes himself look at me, and what he didn't want me to see is the pity which creases his face, reddens his eyes. I slide the newspaper out from under his fingers. I don't want to touch it but I can't let it leave the room: I am in there.

'Well, I should go,' he says, holding his hat against his chest.

I roll the paper under my arm as if I'm only off for a stroll, a smoke. As if it's less than nothing to me. I whistle a little ditty on my way to the window. But the door hasn't shut, he's still in the room.

I grip the paper. 'Shall I see you again?'

'Tomorrow, if I can.'

I try to smile, it sits a little thin. I wave him off instead. The door clicks shut. I sit at the table, my back to the window. I tap the rolled up paper against my chin. Is this it? Am I on my own now they have what they want from me? He says he'll be back but will he? Am I just a story to be finished and put aside?

The paper feels old and dry as my skin; maybe I'm becoming paper too... mustn't think about such things, not now. I shift a little out of my own shadow, spread open the paper. I'm inside those pages, somewhere, someone has written me – forever *that* recorded in black ink. I run my finger along the horizon of each page until I find it.

The drawing – that must be me, the me they saw that day – the dots and lines show an old man in cap and rags, body curled and knotted. I hunch over the paper to read the words. It's so long since I read anything. The letters won't stop jumping, the lines won't separate. I slap my palm over the page. I'm too close, light from the window spills around me at the table. I sit back in the chair, peel away each finger. It's still there, the words, the drawing, of course it is. I feel as small as that square picture in the corner – that Mr Wakefield should have seen me like this, that anyone should.

I stare at the page long enough that the words settle, the lines crawl apart.

They call that sad specimen William Norris, and I'm sorry to my brother for that but pleased no one who knew James Norris would recognise that cap-wearing, withered stick of a creature. The words call me an American seaman, I see them there in front of me but they aren't the truth. I'm a marine, I only ever fought for England though I've spent most of my life at sea and I am a man so some things are as they tell them. But what they say about that cell is true: a trough bed, yes my cot was that, yes there were chains around my neck, my waist... only they don't know all of it, I couldn't even tell Mr Wakefield all. Some things are hidden, chained away, deep inside myself, and should never be let out.

I leave the newspaper open, fluttering in a breeze from the

window. Let that poor creature get some light. Part of me wishes he could creep out of those pages and be away – the other part of me hopes all that doesn't start again.

The only one who might see something of me in those eyes and that broken nose is Ruth, but she wouldn't know for sure, not from our time together when I was a proper man, when my years made me tall and strong, when the sun and the wind browned me, when I was all myself. She won't be able to read the words, or she couldn't read back then. Maybe, since then, she's had a better teacher. I hope many better things have happened to her since me.

Ruth's out there now, maybe biting into an apple, gazing out at the sea, living her life without me. I am without country, without family, without. Yet I smile as sunlight strikes the window.

I should ask for a pencil and some paper. I can do a better drawing. I will draw Ruth.

There's her deep dark eyes. I know every detail. The point of her chin, the curl of her earlobe. I remember it all.

I know her face. I know the arch of her eyebrow, the pale lashes. Her smell of lavender and salt. The curve of her arms, the narrowness of her back. The weight of her breasts, the bumps of her ribs. And aged as she must be, as am I, she will always be beautiful.

I never planned to fall in love, and at the first storm I abandoned ship, let the sails rip free, and love run aground.

Ruth probably wants nothing from me, but I'd like to tell her I'm sorry, and no matter how much I tell myself she deserves that at least, I know it's only for me, and in telling her I hope she'll see I never stopped loving her.

Here's to us, Ruth. Was it all so bad?

50

'Fleet, how was it you came to save me?' I ask.

'Leave off,' Fleet says.

He arrives on time just as he always does. He carries the smell of the market, hot potatoes, cloves and parsley from the butchers, specks of wax from the chandler's shop in his hair. He closes the door behind him, puts his basket on the table. I stay close behind, tap him on the shoulder.

'Did you throw the drowning man a rope, Fleet?'

His cheeks simmer red. He's easy to tease but I see his chest puff up, and it's clear to see he takes pride in all the things he does. He doesn't need to visit me, but he likes to fetch me treats from the market: slices of tongue, wedges of game pie, red apples. These costs come out of his pocket.

'Did you pull down the place brick by brick, Fleet?'

He laughs, shakes his head. 'I just fetch the food and lay the table.'

'Oh, it's much more than that,' I say, and there's no joking about all Fleet has done for me.

He's been at my side since the cell opened. But he saved me long before my Friend the Quaker knocked at Bedlam's door. He brought Davey to me, my companion through the darkest time. Then when I needed him again, Fleet fed me, gave me a blanket, washed my face and feet, led the government to me.

I sit at the table, running over those carvings. *T, B, I*? He opens the basket. The same measuring stick that has seen me become grey, thin, near toothless, has made him plump, egg-shaped. See how time runs up and down like sand in a watchglass. I hope there are more than a few grains left for me.

I glance at the clock on the shelf. It's stopped, or I'm back all those years ago – ten, fourteen – too many to remember.

Fleet collects up the clock. He flicks the glass, the hands twitch then fall back. 'I'll get it seen to,' he says.

I shake my head. 'Can't take it with me on the road.'

'I didn't know.'

Maybe he thought I'd always be here, to fetch for, to play with – but that's a mean spirited old bastard speaking, not me. 'Not for yet a while, though.' I soften my voice, 'Not when you're taking such good care of me.'

Fleet nods. 'When you've got your strength back.'

An ungrateful wretch that's what I am. But I have somewhere to be. I owe Mr Wakefield, and Fleet, so much already, wouldn't ask them for the price of the trip. I hope I remember how to read the stars; Fletcher taught me long ago, and how to live with their company.

I get down the plates and cups, set the table. A pie and apples. In the cell I would have torn out a man's eyes for such a feast, even just to look at it, to feel the shine, the warmth, but these days I find I haven't the stomach for food. Fleet has appetite enough for us both.

I tap the chair for him to join me. He peels both apples,

divides them up, pushes the knife back into his pocket. It seems I'm not to be trusted with a blade.

He holds up a long curl of apple peel. 'Good luck,' he says.

I say, 'I'm through with luck.' I go to the window, lay my palm on the cool glass. 'I don't hope for anything but the chance to tell Ruth I was wrong.'

'I could ask her to come –'

'Don't tell anyone.'

He shakes his head, holds up his hands, lets the peel fall to the table. 'Where will you go?'

'She's out there. Wales, I'm sure.' I speak to Fleet as I spoke to myself in the cell.

Fleet glances at the door. 'That's no more than a few hours ride.'

Like any land lover, he's no head for distances. 'It's a lifetime, but I'm not done yet.'

'Does she expect you?'

'Somewhere deep inside, I hope so.'

Maybe I've said too much of Ruth and my plan but it feels good to speak of it out loud. We share the pie and apples, though Fleet eats most of it. And as he talks, and eats, and waves his hands, jigs his feet under the table, I notice something out of the corner of my eye. It's only a flicker, like a mouse darting out of sight. I shake it from my thoughts. I try to eat, try to keep my gaze on the white apple flesh.

The earthy smell of the pie, I will think on that.

Fleet stands by the door. I didn't see him get up. He holds the basket against his chest. 'I'll get the clock fixed.' He takes a key out of his pocket. 'Just to keep the newspaper men out,' he says, locking the door behind him.

I rest the side of my head against the door.

'Fleet,' I say.

'Yes?' he answers from the other side.

'This here's still Bethlem, ain't it?'

'It is.'

'I have to go to her.'

The lock clicks open, the door stays shut. 'Goodbye,' Fleet says.

'Huryl fawr – go with the wind in your sails, friend.'

It sounds deep and hollow out there like holding a seashell to my ear. My legs shake, my head pounds. I'm leaving. I'll go tonight, with the first sight of a star.

I should lie down, get some rest before then, my guts twist and ache. I press myself against the back of the chair; the pain in my gut keeps me awake. And I'm thankful for that. Never know what might be waiting when I close my eyes. I press my hands against my stomach.

A curl of apple skin sits on the table shining like brass. Golden ribbons for Ruth. Black hair, those gold threads of hair and ribbon catching bright sparks in the lamp light. Salt on my lips. A forest of masts out on the water. The rock of the boat, the weight of our bodies, entwined together, holding us steady. We'd hidden amongst the stowed sails. And when the rain fell on deck, we heard it but didn't feel it. We were hidden inside each other.

Try to breathe but only blood bubbles on my lips. I push back, fall against the table. The pain comes again, lower, deeper down.

I drag the pot out from under the bed, drop my breeches. I crouch, squeezing my knees; biting my lip to hold back the scream. I strain, eyes ready to burst out of my head. Legs and arms shaking.

Nothing comes out of me.

I stand, wince as feeling returns to my legs. Peering down, I see it.

Down between my feet, in the bottom of the pot, a silvery flash... Spittle of mucusy blood. It twitches. Can't turn away. Slowly bone, flesh, skin, knits itself together. Something is being born.

I kick the pot. It skids under the bed, out of sight.

Can't rub it from my eyes. The flicker is brighter now, like a signal from a passing ship. Shining out from under the blanket. It tries to make me look. It will blind me with its brightness if I do.

How did it get under the bed? Maybe it came from the basket. Maybe it's only dust and cobweb stuck together.

But I know those things aren't the truth of it.

I make myself look again, squinting against the flashes of light; let the monster come...

The room darkens, clouds drawing over the windowpanes. There's a scratching noise under the bed. A wet splattering sound slithers out from under the mattress; it sounds like rain falling on the main deck. I put my hands over my ears.

The echo of small gasps, smacking lips, vibrates through the bed and into me. I shuffle to the edge, peer into the thick blue gloom. Something shiny flickers in the piss pot, a tiny glistening glob.

It twitches.

The silver burns brighter than lit gun-powder. I see its fiery outline before me even when I close my eyes. But I have to watch.

A burning triangle flapping, growing, scales dazzling as pearls. It births itself into a mackerel. Rainbow colours lighting up the bed, spilling out over the floor. One golden eye stares out at me. I bend down. It flips over, wriggles upright. I thought once it was a monster, but it's not that.

The light drips from its eyes, puddles at my feet. We watch each other. No words, no movement but the quiver of its gills, the rise and fall of my chest. We are together in this bright moment. Skin and scales. Gills and mouth.

Outside the evening crashes at the window, splashing against the glass, spiralling waves fill the street, but it is light as midday around us. The mackerel flips out of the pot, lands on my boot.

'Been waiting long?' I ask.

'I never gave up on you,' the mackerel replies.

51

'Breathe. Breathe. Keep breathing,' the mackerel says.

The sea sweeps about my chest, embracing me. She jumps and splashes, at home here in the water. Me, I'm used to being on the surface.

She asks, 'Trust me?'

'I think I do.'

The stones beneath my feet shift and settle, smooth and cool as glass. Dawn flares pink on the horizon. I turn back to land. Portsmouth Docks. 'Where will we go?'

'All must pass through the Solent. Will you follow me?'

I call out as I dive, 'Come, who's for blue water?' The sea wraps itself around me...

He's a fever. See how he sweats.

... There is no air, no need for air. I swim with the mackerel, gliding in her wake, as good as floating. We travel over shipwrecks, masts, bottles, wheels, all peeking from the silt and sand – wishing us safe voyage. The colours, blues, greens, yellows, brighter than holding coloured glass to the sun. Blinding but beautiful. I have no fear of losing my way.

We're rounding Spithead. The bright sandbank, the hulls, rising above us, pierce the sunlight. On the glassy surface bodies form from the whiteness – hair, eyes, features. My face stares back, my younger self, and beside that young man I was is Ruth. She laughs, wipes her mouth on the back of her hand. The young me pats her back. I feel it again now, charging through the water, as the mackerel leaps and twists, the lightening strike of love. I try to reach the surface, legs kicking, but the current is too strong, hauling me further out to sea. They are still up there in the distance, yet to be reached.

A swirl of bubbles, and out in the English Channel. In the far distance Wales, swept along by St George's Channel. A small boat hops and skips across the waves, buoyed by youthful hope. If I were closer I'd call a warning, tell that young girl to keep sailing close to home.

The mackerel asks, 'How would she ever reach you?'

'I'm not worth reaching.'

'He who has no faults is not born.'

I smile at hearing Ruth's words in such a creature's mouth. 'People do as people do, I suppose.'

'This way. Keep up.'

And we burst out into the cool rush of the Atlantic. A deepness so far below that there is no end to it. An all-swallowing darkness, but above us the light, the sun at full height, burning in its own blue expanse of sky. The hulk of a shadow glides over us, bigger than any whale. An eighty-gun ship of the line going by the depth of its seat in the water. I'm small as a barnacle down here beneath it. Soon out the other side.

Midnight on the water, each man is his own shadow – as is the way in life – the lamp-lit deck is bright white as boiled bones. Gulls circle the masts, looking for rest, crying out to the boy skylarking in the rigging. He doesn't hear them.

Higher, higher, the boy goes. Smaller, smaller, we race away.

Fletcher is the one up there. He turns his head. Does he see me, a flash of something deep below? I see him falling but not fallen. I know he waits for me to open my arms and catch him. I see my brother falling from the tree just as happened when we were children. The honeyed scent of windfall apples, the flinty lure of arrowheads, the tang of sweat from walking, the fizzing excitement of breaking rules.

He floats, arms out like wings, shirt fluttering. He floats.

On, and on, warmed by the Gulf Stream. In and out of its heated spots that feel like joy, and cold spots, chill as sadness, passing through each to the other side; but they can't be washed away, they latch to us like weeds and mussels to a hull and even if a ship keeps sailing they will slow it to a halt in the end. The mackerel's fins slice fast through the water, bearing us onwards.

'Where?' I ask.

'To the beginning of all that and the end of all this,' she says.

The sun sets with a hiss. Surrounded by redness like blood in the water. A bucket emptied over the side after a flogging. The screams of salt on flayed skin echo deep down in the heart of the ocean. Ripples surround us, making the mackerel scales flutter like leaves on an apple tree. It's a hollowing out from the guts to the toes. Marines, hold position.

I can take any pain…

Call the surgeon, Fleet. He needs help.
His stomach is like stone.
Crowther won't come.
Get Rodley to force him if needed. There must be something we can do.

… Closer to shore now, silt and mud churns below. The brackish taste of fresh water, rivers draining into the sea. The cries of birds.

'Let me take the pain – I can take it all.'

'It is coming,' the mackerel says, circling about me. 'No holding it back.'

All life rushes above. A calmness inside, the warmth of the water seeping into my blood. Swirling through night now, it rises from the mud to fill the hole left by the setting sun.

Thick as tar, suspended, arms and legs held aloft.

No mackerel, no sea. But I'm not alone.

A beating in my ears, a pulsing rhythm. Shapes loom close, speckled with light like looking at the world through a blanket. Currents rush past, whooshing, caressing.

A hand comes towards me. Interlocked fingers before my face, red light shining between. I try to reach them, throw out my hand, kick with my foot, but we are separated by a tight drum of skin. A laugh ripples through the water.

My mother's voice. 'We're waiting,' she whispers.

I am me, will always be me.

I'm floating inside, inside the beautiful inside…

You can't bleed him anymore, Crowther.

You dragged me here. Where's Haslam? Thinks he's so important. Don't see him curing this one.

Help him.

... Think perhaps I've yet to be born. Waiting, out there is the shore of a new world that's ancient as the ocean. My mother sinks herself into the water. The cold is thrilling after so much heat. The pond feeds into a creek which flows into the sea. We are part of that ebb.

The greenness of the water, the sleekness of the reeds, the feel of silky silt, the nibble of minnows, it is familiar after all her new beginnings. She dips her ears under the water, closes her eyes, floats on her back. No shimmering hummingbirds, no trailing partridgeberry plants. She can pretend she's back at Frensham Ponds, at home in Farnham. But this is where she belongs now, here in New England, with a new life. Though it feels as if she's always known this child inside her, knows it will be a boy, knows she'll feel the comfort of his hands when she is old and he is a man.

She laughs, locks her arms about us.

We cool, we float, we slow.

Where my son was, I am again.

'I can't wait to meet you,' whispers my mother. 'Don't hold on too long.'

And I have been holding on too long.

A beat, booming this time, stronger even than her heart, coming from unfathomable depths, no need to reach out, it comes again, a throbbing, a tingling, a tight cradling.

It comes for me.

I let go.